A PRICE
BEYOND

BY
CAROLE MORTIMER

MILLS & BOON

Published in Great Britain 2014
by Mills & Boon, an imprint of Harlequin (UK) Limited,
Eton House, 18-24 Paradise Road, Richmond, Surrey, TW9 1SR

© 2014 Carole Mortimer

ISBN: 978 0 263 90831 2

Harlequin (UK) Limited's policy is to use papers that are natural, renewable and recyclable products and made from wood grown in sustainable forests. The logging and manufacturing processes conform to the legal environmental regulations of the country of origin.

Printed and bound in Spain
by Blackprint CPI, Barcelona

Carole Mortimer was born in England, the youngest of three children. She began writing in 1978, and has now written over one hundred and fifty books for Harlequin Mills & Boon®. Carole has six sons: Matthew, Joshua, Timothy, Michael, David and Peter. She says, 'I'm happily married to Peter senior; we're best friends as well as lovers, which is probably the best recipe for a successful relationship. We live in a lovely part of England.' Carole loves to hear from her readers. She can be reached at contact@carolemortimer.co.uk, or her website www.carolemortimer.co.uk

Recent titles by the same author:

A BARGAIN WITH THE ENEMY
  (The Devilish D'Angelos)
RUMOURS ON THE RED CARPET
  (Scandal in the Spotlight)
A TOUCH OF NOTORIETY
A TASTE OF THE FORBIDDEN
  (Buenos Aires Nights)

Did you know these are also available as eBooks?
Visit www.millsandboon.co.uk

For Peter, as always.

PROLOGUE

St Mary's Church, London.

'IT'S NOT TOO late, Gabe,' Rafe drawled softly. The church was packed with his brother's softly chatting wedding guests as they waited for the bride to arrive.

'I checked earlier. There's a door at the back of the vestry where you can escape...'

'Shut up, Rafe.' His two brothers, one seated either side of Rafe, spoke together; Gabriel with the tension of the anxious bridegroom, and Michael with his customary terseness.

'Hush, Rafe.' Their father spoke with soft warning from the pew behind them.

Rafe grinned unrepentantly. 'The jet is just sitting there on the tarmac at the airport, Gabe, and instead of flying off to the Caribbean for your honeymoon, you could just get the hell out of Dodge.'

'Will you just stop?' Gabriel turned to glare at him, his face white and strained as he waited for the start of the organ music that would announce the arrival of his bride at the church. Bryn was already five minutes late, and each minute had seemed like an hour, deepening the lines of tension in his brow.

Rafe's grin widened as he relaxed back in the pew,

having long considered teasing both of his brothers as being part of his role in life.

'You and Michael would never have had any adventures at all if it weren't for me!'

'Marriage to Bryn is going to be biggest adventure of my life,' Gabriel assured him with certainty.

Rafe was aware of how many years his brother had been in love with Bryn, a love his brother had believed was doomed to remain unrequited until just a short month ago.

'She's gorgeous, I'll admit that.'

'Rafe, will you just stop winding him up?' Michael, the eldest of the three brothers, clipped abruptly as Gabriel's hands clenched and unclenched. 'We don't need a fist fight between the groom and one of the best men to liven up the proceedings!'

'I was only—' Rafe broke off as the ringtone of his mobile jarred loudly in the relative silence of the church.

'I told you to switch that damned thing off before you came into the church!' Gabriel turned on him fiercely, obviously relieved to have something tangible to vent his tension on.

'I thought I had.' Rafe grimaced as he pulled the slim mobile from the breast pocket of his morning jacket and quickly turned it to silent mode before slipping it back in his pocket. 'But seriously, Gabe, you still have time to slip out the back of the church and make your escape before anyone is any the wiser.'

'Raphael Charles D'Angelo!'

Rafe winced, having absolutely no idea how his mother, very petite at all of five feet tall, still managed to silence each and every one of her three six-foot-plus sons, all aged in their thirties, with just their full name spoken in that particularly reproving tone of voice!

Although he was thankfully saved from having to turn and face further admonishment from her as the organ played out the wedding march, announcing Bryn's arrival.

The tension instantly eased from Gabriel's shoulders as the three brothers stood up.

Rafe winced as he felt the vibration of his mobile against his chest to announce another incoming call. He chose to ignore it as he turned to look at Bryn as she walked slowly down the aisle on her stepfather's arm.

'Oh, wow, Gabe, Bryn looks absolutely stunning,' he breathed sincerely. Bryn a vision in white lace and satin, the glow of her smile as she looked down the aisle at Gabriel enough to light up the whole church.

'Of course she does,' Gabriel murmured smugly, an expression of adoration on his face as he gazed at the woman he loved more than life itself.

'Who the hell would be crass enough to phone you during your own brother's wedding?' Michael demanded critically as he joined Rafe to one side of where the wedding guests now stood outside the church in the summer sunshine, watching indulgently as the bride and groom were photographed together. Both Gabriel and Bryn were glowing with happiness.

Rafe grimaced as he looked up from checking his mobile; this was the first occasion he'd had to look for any messages. 'Just a friend calling to warn me that Monique is on the warpath since she found out I won't be returning to Paris after the wedding.'

The three brothers rotated the management of the three privately owned and world-renowned Archangel galleries and auction houses. Michael would be taking over from Rafe at the Paris gallery on Monday, Gabe was to be based in London once he had returned from his honeymoon, and Rafe was flying to New York tomorrow to take over the gallery there.

'You couldn't have just told her that before you left?' Michael barked irritably.

Rafe shrugged. 'I thought I had.'

'Obviously she didn't get the message.' Michael scowled before turning to look over at Gabriel and Bryn between narrowed lids. 'Can you believe our little brother is now a married man?'

Rafe gave an affectionate grin as he also looked over at the happy couple. 'And obviously loving every minute of it!' And Gabriel wasn't such a 'little' brother to them either, only two years younger than Michael's thirty-five, and one year younger than Rafe's thirty-four.

As well as being close in age, the three brothers were alike in their appearance and colouring: all tall and ruggedly handsome, with ebony-dark hair, brown eyes, and olive-toned skin, all courtesy of their Italian grandfather.

Michael was the remote and austere brother, preferring to keep his ebony hair styled short, his eyes so deep brown they appeared piercing black, and just as unfathomable as the man behind those eyes.

Gabriel was quietly but lethally determined, his hair curling about his ears and nape, his eyes a warm chocolate-brown.

Meanwhile Rafe kept his hair styled well below his collar, and much longer than either of his two brothers, and his eyes were so light brown that they glowed with the gold of a predator. He was also considered by most to be the least serious of the three D'Angelo brothers. At least by those who didn't really know him well; those that did were fully aware that Rafe was just as steely as his two brothers beneath that outwardly flirtatious and teasing manner.

Michael raised mocking brows. 'I take it that Monique wasn't the one for you, any more than the rest of the legion of women you've been involved with over the last fifteen years?'

Rafe gave his brother a pitying look. 'I'm not looking for "the one", thank you very much!'

Michael smiled slightly. 'One of these days she might just find you!'

'Hah, in your dreams.' Rafe chuckled. 'I accept that Gabe is ecstatically happy with Bryn, but I don't for one minute believe in that "one love of your life" thing when it comes to myself. Any more than you do,' he added knowingly.

'No,' his brother confirmed emphatically, his eyes an unreadable black. 'I'm not going to be plagued with telephone calls and visits from this Monique woman when I get to Paris, am I, pleading with me to tell her where you are and how she can contact you?'

'I hope not.' Rafe sighed wearily. 'We had fun for a few weeks, but now it's over.'

Michael gave a shake of his head, his expression one of irritation.

'She doesn't seem to realise that.' He gave Rafe a hard stare. 'Perhaps you could turn your charm onto something more useful once you get to New York? Dmitri Palitov's daughter will be coming to the gallery on Tuesday,' he explained at Rafe's questioning look. 'She's personally overseeing the installation of the display cabinets she designed for her father's jewellery exhibition at the gallery next weekend. She will be staying for the duration of the exhibition, along with Palitov's own security.'

Rafe's eyes widened disbelievingly. 'What the hell?'

'Palitov wanting his own security is understandable.' His brother gave a brief shrug. 'Allowing his daughter to design the display cabinets and her continued presence at the gallery before and during the exhibition were also conditions for Palitov agreeing to there being an exhibition at all.'

Rafe was as aware as Michael that it was a coup for the Archangel gallery that the reclusive Russian billionaire had agreed to allow his private collection to be exhibited at all. No one but Dmitri Palitov had seen the majority of that jewellery for decades, some of it reputed to have belonged to the Tsarina herself, after it had disappeared from Russia last century.

'I'm relying on you to keep the daughter sweet for the next few weeks,' Michael added.

'What exactly does that mean?' Rafe frowned incredulously. 'Palitov is pushing eighty, so how old is his daughter?'

'Does it matter how old she is?' Michael dismissed uninterestedly. 'I'm not asking you to sleep with her, just use some of that lethal Raphael D'Angelo charm on her,' his brother drawled mockingly before giving Rafe a patronising pat on the back and strolling away to join their parents.

Rafe gave a disgusted huff, not at all happy at being expected to use his charm on the middle-aged daughter of a reclusive Russian billionaire.

CHAPTER ONE

Three days later. The Archangel gallery, New York.

'WOULD YOU MIND moving? I'm afraid you're in the way.'

Rafe straightened in the doorway of the east gallery of Archangel, where he had been standing for the past few minutes observing the installation of the glass and bronze cabinets being brought in for the displaying of the Palitov jewellery collection. He turned now to look at the young lad who had just spoken to him so abruptly.

He seemed to be in his teens, and a couple of inches under six feet tall, dressed in the same faded denims and bulky black sweatshirt as the other workers, and wearing a baseball cap pulled low over his face.

A face that was a little too pretty for a boy, Rafe realised: arched dark brows above eyes the green of fresh moss, and surrounded by long and thick dark lashes, a pert nose with a light smattering of freckles, high cheekbones above hollow cheeks, with full and lush lips above a pointed and determined chin.

Yes, he was a bit too pretty, Rafe acknowledged ruefully, although he didn't seem to be having any trouble helping to wheel the display cases into place.

Rafe had arrived at the gallery at eight-thirty as usual, only to learn from his assistant manager that the Palitov crew had been here since eight o'clock. 'I was just looking for—'

'If you wouldn't mind moving now?' the boy repeated huskily. 'We really need to bring in the rest of the display cabinets.' Two of the more burly workmen had moved to stand beside and slightly behind the younger man, as if to emphasise the point.

Rafe frowned his irritation with that muscled presence; where the hell was Dmitri Palitov's daughter?

Those green eyes widened as Rafe still made no effort to shift out of the doorway. 'I don't believe your employer would approve of your lack of cooperation.'

'It so happens I'm only here because I'm looking for your employer,' Rafe replied in frustration.

A wary expression now entered those long-lashed dark green eyes. 'You are?'

'I am,' Rafe confirmed with a hard smile. 'It was my understanding that Miss Palitov would be here herself this morning to oversee the installation of the display cabinets.' He raised mocking and pointed brows.

The boy looked even less certain of himself now. 'And you are?'

His mouth thinned with satisfaction. 'Raphael D'Angelo.'

The boy winced. 'I had a feeling you might be.' The youth straightened. 'Good morning, Mr D'Angelo. I'm Nina Palitov,' she added as he made no effort to take her outstretched hand.

Nina had the satisfaction of seeing the man she now knew to be Raphael D'Angelo, one of the three brothers who owned the prestigious Archangel galleries, briefly lose some of his obviously inborn arrogance as those golden eyes widened with disbelief, the sculptured lips parting in surprise.

It gave Nina the chance to study the man standing in

front of her. He was probably in his mid-thirties, or possibly a little younger, with long and silky ebony-dark hair styled rakishly to just below his shoulders, and with the face of a fallen angel. He had predatory golden eyes, sharp blades for cheekbones beneath that olive-toned skin, his nose long and aristocratic, sensuous lips that looked as if they had been lovingly chiselled by a sculptor, his jaw square—and at the moment tilted at an arrogantly challenging angle.

The perfectly tailored charcoal-grey suit and snowy white shirt did nothing to hide the muscled perfection of his taller than average frame—rather, it had no doubt been tailored to emphasise that masculinity! A suit that Nina belatedly realised had probably cost as much as a month's rent on any number of exclusive Manhattan penthouse apartments. The white shirt was of the finest silk, as was the pale silver tie knotted so meticulously at his throat, and his black leather shoes were obviously of the finest Italian leather.

As if all of that weren't enough of an indication of who he was, that softly modulated and educated English accent should have been the giveaway, added to which this man's olive complexion showed he was obviously of Italian descent.

Nina's gaze swept back up to that arrogant—and breathtakingly handsome—face. 'I'm guessing from your expression that I'm not quite what you were expecting, Mr D'Angelo?' she murmured ruefully.

Not what Rafe was expecting?

That had to be the understatement of the decade; it was bad enough that he had thought he was talking to a too-pretty boy, but discovering that boy was in fact a beautiful young woman, and Dmitri Palitov's daughter, was a little hard to accept. Palitov was almost eighty years old, and the woman now claiming to be Nina Palitov could only be in her mid-twenties at the most.

Or maybe Nina was Palitov's granddaughter, and for some reason was here in place of her mother?

Rafe forced the tension to ease from his shoulders.

'Not what, who,' he excused lightly, deciding to keep the 'pretty boy' mistake to himself as he finally briefly shook the hand she held out to him. A warm and artistically slender hand, the fingers long and delicately tapered, the nails kept short.

She looked up at him quizzically with those moss-green eyes. 'And exactly who were you expecting, Mr D'Angelo?'

'Your mother, probably,' Rafe dismissed dryly. 'Or possibly your aunt?'

She gave a rueful smile. 'My mother is dead, and I don't have an aunt. Or an uncle, either,' she added dryly as Rafe would have spoken again. 'Or any other family apart from my father,' she said softly.

Rafe blinked, eyes narrowing as he attempted to process the information this woman had just given him. No mother, no aunts or uncles, just her father. Which meant...

'I'm the Miss Palitov you were told to expect, Mr D'Angelo,' she confirmed huskily. 'I believe I'm what some people might describe as being a child born in the autumn years of my father's life.'

And Rafe would be one of those people!

He'd had no idea that Dmitri Palitov's daughter would be so young. Had Michael known? Probably not, otherwise his brother would never have suggested that Rafe charm her! It was unusual for his big brother not to have all the facts, but this just went to prove that not even the meticulous Michael was infallible.

And this woman's identity probably also explained those two muscle-bound men now standing as silent and watchful sentinels at Nina Palitov's back. No doubt Daddy Palitov kept a very close guard over his young and beautiful daughter.

As if those bodyguards, and the information that this young woman was Dmitri Palitov's daughter, weren't disconcerting enough, she now reached up and swept the baseball cap from her head, releasing a waterfall of fiery red curls that framed the beauty of her face and cascaded over the slenderness of her shoulders before flowing riotously down almost to her waist.

And leaving Rafe in absolutely no doubt that she was a woman.

Rafe's preference in women had always been towards pocket-sized blondes, but as he saw the rueful amusement—at his expense—in those moss-green eyes, the slightly mocking curve to those lushly full lips, evidence, no doubt, that Nina Palitov found his discomfort amusing, he knew that he would enjoy nothing more at this moment than to take this beautiful woman in his arms before kissing that amusement from the sweet curve of those lush and pouting lips.

A move on his part that would no doubt cause those two muscle-bound sentinels to move with lightning speed in her defence.

Nina eyed Raphael D'Angelo beneath lowered lashes, knowing, by the glance he briefly gave at Rich and Andy as they stood behind her, that he had now realised helping to move display cases wasn't their only reason for being at the Archangel gallery.

She had been surrounded by the same bodyguards for most of her life, had grown so accustomed to having at least two of them watch over her day and night that she rarely noticed they were there any more. She now treated the eight men who made up her security detail more like friends than people employed by her father to ensure her safety.

Which was a sad reflection on what her life had become, Nina realised with a frown.

Admittedly her father was a wealthy and powerful man, and Nina knew better than most that with that wealth and power came enemies. But she had often thought wistfully of how nice it would be to be able to do as other people her age did, and just pop out to collect the newspaper or a carton of milk in the mornings, or a takeaway for dinner from a fast-food restaurant, or share a fun evening out with several girlfriends, without her bodyguards having to check out the venue first.

Or maybe go out for a date with an arrogant and decadently handsome man with the face of a fallen angel.

And exactly where had that ridiculous thought come from?

The long years of her father's protection meant that Nina was usually extremely shy when it came to talking to men; she certainly never had erotic fantasies about them the first time she met them!

She frowned up at Raphael D'Angelo, a man who could never be considered as being anything other than an arrogant and decadently handsome man with the face of a fallen angel.

'I have a lot to do here today, Mr D'Angelo,' she told him, hiding her shyness behind the briskness of her tone. 'So if there was nothing else?'

Rafe knew when he was being dismissed. And he also knew when he didn't like it!

He was in charge of the New York gallery at the moment, and it was time that Miss Nina Palitov and those muscle-bound goons standing behind her were made aware of that fact.

'There are a few things I would like to discuss with you first, if you would care to accompany me up to my office on the third floor?'

The blinking of those long dark lashes was the only evidence that she was surprised by his request. No doubt Daddy's money and power ensured that Miss Nina Palitov rarely, if ever, acceded to anyone's request for her to do anything.

Her expression was wistful as she gave a predictable shake of her head, causing that long cascade of fiery red hair to shimmer like a living flame in the sunlight pouring in through the floor-to-ceiling windows behind her.

'I obviously don't have time at the moment. Perhaps later on this morning?'

Rafe's mouth tightened.

'I have several other appointments to deal with today.' But none, he knew, that Michael, at least, wouldn't expect him to cancel in favour of meeting with Dmitri Palitov's daughter, whenever it was convenient for her.

But Michael wasn't here right now, Rafe was, and—

Hell, just admit it, Rafe—the reason you're so damned irritated is because Nina Palitov is utterly gorgeous. And under other circumstances, in a different location—the two of them naked together in a silk-sheeted bed came to mind—he might even enjoy the challenge she represented, both sexually and to his authority.

But they weren't in a bed, that lush mouth wasn't his for the taking, and when it came to Archangel he was the one in charge.

She shrugged dismissively. 'In that case, I'm afraid the discussion will have to wait until tomorrow.'

Rafe took a step closer to her, only to find that the two

men standing behind Nina Palitov took that same step forward, flanking her closely now as they both watched him between narrowed eyes.

'Call off your watchdogs,' he advised harshly.

She eyed him frowningly for several long seconds before slowly turning her head to look at the two men. 'I'm sure Mr D'Angelo poses absolutely no threat to me,' she assured them wryly before turning back to once again look challengingly at Rafe.

As if she believed his wealth and power also rendered him over-indulged and wimpish, a man who wouldn't stand a chance against these two muscle-bound men if they were to take exception to something he said or did.

Admittedly, the two of them together might be pushing it a bit, but Rafe had no doubts that in a one-on-one fight his hours at the gym, and his training in several of the martial arts, would ensure he could best either one of these two men, whether they chose to fight dirty or fair—and their threatening poses indicated it would probably be the former.

He forced the tension from his shoulders as he gave a deliberately wolfish smile as his appreciative gaze swept slowly over Nina Palitov.

'Oh, I wouldn't go so far as to say that I posed absolutely no threat to you, Miss Palitov,' he purred softly, his tone deliberately provocative.

Those beautiful moss-green eyes widened noticeably, a delicate blush creeping into her peaches-and-cream cheeks, and succeeding in making the endearing freckles on the bridge of her nose appear more prominent. At the same time her tongue flicked out nervously to moisten the lushness of those delectably plump lips. Lips that had no need for lip gloss to enhance their fullness or deliciously peach colour.

Those lips thinned now, as if Nina Palitov was well aware that Rafe was playing with her, and she didn't appreciate it.

'Would eleven o'clock be convenient to you, Mr D'Angelo?' she bit out huskily.

'I'll make sure that it is,' he drawled softly.

Nina was very aware that somewhere during the course of this exchange Raphael D'Angelo had taken control of the conversation—and her? His air of lazy confidence and power implied that he preferred always to be in control.

Even when he was in bed with a woman?

Nina felt the colour warm her cheeks for a second time in as many minutes as she realised that Raphael D'Angelo was responsible for bringing those totally inappropriate thoughts into her head.

Why were they so inappropriate?

She was twenty-four years old, with a slender figure, and the way men looked at her told her she wasn't unattractive. And Raphael D'Angelo was dangerously, overwhelmingly handsome in a swarthily Latin way that she realised made her nerve-endings sizzle. They were both over twenty-one, so why shouldn't she indulge in a little light flirtation with him?

Because it wasn't something she was accustomed to doing, came the instant, and sad, reply. Her father was very protective of her, claustrophobically so at times, and it was a little difficult to enjoy a flirtation with an attractive man with two bodyguards always standing at her back. Especially when those same two bodyguards would no doubt report that behaviour back to her father if necessary.

Besides, she might have only just met him for the first time, but it was long enough to know that Raphael

D'Angelo really was too dangerous a man for Nina to practise her relatively inexperienced flirtation skills on.

She knew his reputation, of course; even she had heard the New York gossip about this particular D'Angelo brother, enough to know that Raphael D'Angelo's relationships with women were brief and numerous, and that there was no such thing as a light flirtation where this particular man was concerned.

'Do that.' Nina nodded abruptly, her defensive hackles rising.

Those golden eyes narrowed to steely slits. 'I believe, as it seems we will be required to spend a certain amount of time together over the next few weeks, that you will find me to be much more amenable to your needs if our relationship is one based on mutual respect.'

Nina blinked. 'It's been my experience that respect is earned rather than a given.'

His jaw tightened. 'Meaning?'

Nina kept her expression deliberately blank. 'I don't believe there was any hidden meaning to my comment, Mr D'Angelo, merely a statement of fact.'

Rafe doubted that very much.

Damn, but this woman was irritating. Cool, detached— and damned irritating!

She was also beautiful, in an exotically unusual way; a man could drown in those deep moss-green eyes, become lost in caressing the smooth softness of her skin, and as for those lush and kissable lips? Rafe had no idea what her breasts were like, of course, hidden as they were beneath that bulky black sweatshirt, but her hips and thighs were slender, her legs so long they seemed to go on for ever. As for that abundance of long and curling silkily soft hair, Rafe couldn't ever remember seeing hair of quite that fiery colour before, natural golden and russet highlights visible amongst the red as her sunlit hair surrounded her face like a halo.

Yes, Nina Palitov was all of those things: irritating, beautiful, and desirable—and completely out of any man's reach, if the two heavies standing guard behind her were any indication. And they so obviously were; both men were still eyeing him suspiciously.

She was also, most tellingly of all, the daughter of Dmitri Palitov, the powerful billionaire who took the term reclusive to a whole new level!

She nodded now. 'Obviously I would like the gallery's security to be part of our conversation.'

Rafe looked at her through narrowed lids. 'Archangel's security is my concern, Miss Palitov, not yours.'

She gave a shrug. 'I suggest you read clause seven of the contract your brother Michael signed with my father, Mr D'Angelo. I believe you will find that particular clause states that I have the final say in all security provided for the gallery during the showing of my father's unique jewellery collection.'

What on earth?

Michael had mentioned that Palitov intended to supply his own security for the collection, but at no time had he even suggested that included all of the gallery's security.

Having arrived in New York only the day before, Rafe hadn't yet had time to look in any detail at the contract Archangel had signed with Dmitri Palitov. He had trusted Michael to have dealt with it with his usual ruthless efficiency.

But if what Nina Palitov claimed was true, and Rafe had no reason to believe that it wasn't, then he needed to have a little chat with his big brother.

Admittedly the exhibition of the Palitov jewellery was a coup for Archangel, it would be a coup for any gallery, when the much-coveted collection had never been shown in public before, but that didn't mean they had to allow the Palitov family to just walk in here and take over the whole damned place.

Nina had to hold back a smile as she easily read the frustration in Raphael D'Angelo's expression, inwardly knowing she felt a certain sense of satisfaction in having managed to pierce the confidence of this arrogant man. Raphael D'Angelo was so obviously a man used to issuing orders and having them obeyed without question, and she could see his discomfort now in having been so totally wrong-footed.

And no doubt he would have something to say to his older brother, when next the two men spoke, regarding the concessions Michael D'Angelo had been required to make in order to be able to exhibit her father's jewellery collection.

Nina perfectly understood her father's caution; he had collected the unique and priceless jewellery over many years, and as such it was completely irreplaceable.

'Do you intend trying to change the terms of that contract? If so, perhaps we should call a halt to bringing in any more display cases until after you've spoken with my father?'

'I don't believe I mentioned changing the terms of the contract, Miss Palitov,' Raphael D'Angelo bit out harshly.

'Nina,' she invited softly.

'Rafe,' he countered, golden eyes glittering angrily.

Rafe.

Yes, the shortened version, the rakish version, of this man's name suited him far more than the more formal Raphael.

'Nor do I react well to threats, Nina,' he drawled softly.

'I believe you will find I made a statement rather than

a threat, Rafe,' she replied just as ultra-politely. 'As I also believe you will find that the contract between my father and your brother is completely binding on both sides.'

Nina had been present on the day Michael D'Angelo had met with her father at his Manhattan apartment, both men also having their lawyers present in order to check the details of the contract before it was signed by both of them. Her father never left anything to chance, and the safety of his beloved jewellery collection came second only to his protection of Nina.

'If you have any reservations or doubts, then I suggest it might be preferable if you take them up with your brother before speaking to my father,' she added challengingly.

She had no idea what it was about Raphael, or rather Rafe, D'Angelo that made her bristle so defensively. So uncharacteristically. That arrogant confidence perhaps? Or maybe it was the fact that he was just too dangerously handsome for his own—and any woman's—good? Whatever the reason, Nina found herself wanting to challenge him in a way she never had any other man.

Rafe had more than 'reservations' where Nina Palitov was concerned. Where his attraction to her was concerned.

But he certainly didn't doubt her claim regarding the contract and the security of her father's collection. He knew from the steadiness of that unflinching moss-green gaze that Nina Palitov was telling him nothing but the truth about the contract Michael—ergo, Archangel—had signed with her father. Something else Michael hadn't warned him about, and which Rafe intended taking up with his big brother at his earliest convenience.

He nodded abruptly. 'Very well, I'll make the necessary arrangements for you to view the gallery's full security tomorrow.'

'Today would be more convenient.'

Rafe looked down at her through narrowed lids, easily seeing the challenge in those unblinking green eyes. 'Very well, later today,' he ground out tautly.

'Good.' She gave another terse nod. 'I'll see you in your office on the third floor at eleven o'clock.' She turned away dismissively, gathering up the wild abundance of her hair and pushing it back under her baseball cap as she walked over to rejoin her workmen.

The two bodyguards shot Rafe a warning glance before following hot on Nina Palitov's heels.

A totally unnecessary warning, as far as Rafe was concerned.

He had absolutely no interest in deepening his acquaintance with one Miss Nina Palitov. She was beautiful, yes, and those lips definitely begged to be explored in deeper, more sensuous detail, but the presence of the bodyguards said that wasn't going to happen any time soon, and her dismissive attitude towards Rafe wasn't in the least encouraging either.

No, Miss Nina Palitov was not a woman Rafe had any intention of pursuing on a personal basis.

CHAPTER TWO

A DECISION RAFE had serious reason to question when his assistant, Bridget, showed Nina Palitov into his office two hours later!

Rafe had been extremely busy over those two hours, having no intention of being caught wrong-footed again where this young woman was concerned.

His telephone conversation with Michael hadn't been particularly helpful, his brother showing no interest in the fact that Nina Palitov was aged in her twenties rather than middle-aged, as Rafe had assumed she would be. Michael had simply repeated that it was Rafe's duty to keep Miss Palitov sweet.

The Internet had proved a little more helpful regarding Nina Palitov, revealing that she had been born to Dmitri and Anna Palitov when her mother was thirty and her father in his mid-fifties, which now made Nina twenty-four. It also stated that Anna had died five years after Nina was born, but gave no cause for her premature death.

It also listed the schools Nina had attended, after which she had gone on to Stanford University, attaining a degree in art and design, before taking up a position in her father's extensive business empire.

None of which changed the impact the flesh and blood

Nina Palitov had on Rafe when she walked into his office at eleven o'clock.

Somewhere during the course of her morning's work she had removed the bulky black sweatshirt, revealing a close-fitting white T-shirt beneath. The tightness of the material across her breasts also revealed that she wasn't wearing anything beneath that T-shirt. Her breasts were small and pert, and tipped with darker nipples—the same peach colour as her lips?—as they pressed noticeably against that clinging white material, her abdomen silkily slender as the T-shirt finished just short of her low-rise denims.

She had dispensed with the baseball cap again, that over-abundance of fiery red hair a wild cascade onto the narrowness of her shoulders and down the slender length of her spine. A wild and fiery cascade that now made Rafe's fingers itch to touch it.

And the rising, hardening of Rafe's shaft told him his body had decided, completely in contradiction of his earlier decision to stay away from this young woman, that it also liked what it saw.

'Mr D'Angelo?' Nina prompted as he made no effort to get up and greet her but instead remained seated behind the black marble desk placed in front of the windows across the spacious room.

He had removed his jacket and put it on a hanger some time during the morning, his shoulder-length hair an ebony sheen against the white of his silk shirt. As she had suspected earlier, the broadness of his shoulders, muscled width of his chest, and the tautness of his abdomen owed absolutely nothing to the perfect tailoring of his designer label suit.

Nina deliberately looked away from all that blatant maleness to take in the rest of the spaciously elegant office. Floor-to-ceiling windows made up two of the walls of the corner office, cream silk wallpaper adorned the other two, along with several filled bookcases and a bar, with a comfortable seating area in front of the second wall of windows.

All totally in keeping with the luxurious elegance associated with the world-famous Archangel galleries and auction houses. That reputation and the expensive opulence of this gallery were no doubt the reason her father had chosen Archangel as the venue to exhibit his collection.

Even so, Nina knew that her father would not appreciate the lack of manners Raphael D'Angelo was currently exhibiting towards his only daughter.

'Is this an inconvenient time for you, after all?' she questioned coolly as she turned back to look across the marble desk at him.

'Not at all,' he drawled as he finally stood up to turn away and take his jacket from the hanger and shrug it back on over his wide shoulders before facing her fully, dark brows raised over mocking gold eyes. 'Did you decide to dispense with the bodyguards?'

Nina steadily returned that mocking gaze. 'They're standing just on the other side of that door.' She nodded towards the closed door behind her.

Raphael D'Angelo grinned as he leant back against the front of his black marble desk, arms folded across the width of that muscled chest, every inch of him crying out hot, dangerous male, beware.

'Out of consideration for the fact that I pose absolutely no threat to you?'

Out of consideration for the fact that Nina had told Rich and Andy that that was where they were going to wait for her. They hadn't particularly liked it, but Nina had been adamant. Alone in Raphael D'Angelo's office, very aware of his predatory maleness, and that wicked glint once again visible in those golden eyes, she wasn't so sure of her decision.

Rafe D'Angelo was a dangerously attractive man who even Nina knew had the reputation of being something of a rake when it came to women. An outgoing love-'em-and-leave-'em type of man, in fact, and as such he was completely out of Nina's own limited experience with men.

Which, she knew, was the main reason for her brusqueness towards him earlier this morning; she simply had no previous experience of dealing with men as powerfully attractive as Raphael D'Angelo. With any men at all, other than her father and bodyguards, if the truth be told.

Her father had become something of a recluse after her mother died, at the same time as he had become obsessively protective of Nina. That protection, from men like Rich and Andy, meant Nina had only been out on a few dates these past few years. Always with men her father had first approved of, and who had passed the stringent security checks made on them before Nina could so much as accept an invitation from them to even go out for a pizza.

Rafe D'Angelo, charming on the outside but with a steely and determined inner core, didn't seem like a man who would give a damn about whether he passed security checks or not, if he should decide he was interested in a woman.

Not that Nina thought that he ever would be interested in her; she very much doubted she was beautiful or sophisticated enough to arouse the interest of a man as physically attractive and sought after as she knew Rafe

D'Angelo to be. A man who could have any woman he wanted, and usually did.

But Nina knew instinctively, even from her brief acquaintance with him, that Rafe D'Angelo wouldn't give a damn about whether or not he had her father's or anyone else's approval, or be bothered by the fact that Rich and Andy were standing on the other side of his office door, if he should feel the inclination to kiss her—

What on earth was wrong with her?

Anyone would think that she wanted Rafe D'Angelo to find her attractive. To kiss her, even.

Which was ridiculous. She was only at the Archangel gallery in order to oversee the installation and security of her father's jewellery collection, nothing more. The fact that she was so totally aware of everything about Rafe D'Angelo—the silkiness of his overlong dark hair, that predatory glint in those golden eyes, the hard contours of that sculptured and ruggedly handsome face, the muscled strength of his body—was irrelevant, when she had no intention of allowing her attraction to him to go any further. When her father's protection of her wouldn't allow that attraction to go any further.

'I've made arrangements for you to go down to the basement and view our security at twelve o'clock,' Rafe D'Angelo informed her briskly now, the expression in those golden eyes guarded. 'I trust that time is convenient for you?'

'Perfectly, thank you.' Nina nodded coolly. 'You're also aware, once the collection is in place, that there will be two men from my father's own security detail in the east gallery guarding the collection at all times?'

'So I believe.' He nodded tersely.

Her brows rose at his tone. 'You don't approve?'

'It isn't a question of whether or not I approve,' Rafe

rasped. 'But I find it a tad insulting that your father should feel it necessary, if you really want to know,' he added with obvious impatience.

She shrugged. 'I doubt my father suspects that you, or any of your employees, intend to steal the collection.'

'How reassuring!'

Nina thought they had gone as far as they could on that particular subject; there was no way her father would back off on security for his precious jewellery collection, whether Rafe D'Angelo felt insulted or otherwise. 'So, what was it you wished to discuss with me, Mr D'Angelo?' she prompted lightly.

'I thought we had agreed it would be Rafe and Nina?' he reminded dryly. 'Mr D'Angelo makes me sound like my stern older brother.' He grimaced.

Nina raised auburn brows. 'That would be the Michael D'Angelo who visited my father some weeks ago?'

'You were able to recognise him from my description, hmm?' Rafe drawled ruefully.

Nina shrugged narrow shoulders. 'I found him to be polite, if a little...austere.'

That golden gaze narrowed. 'You've actually met my brother Michael?'

Her eyes widened at the sharpness of his tone. 'I was present when he and my father signed the contracts for the exhibition, yes.' She nodded.

What the hell?

Rafe had spoken to Michael just an hour ago, a conversation in which his brother hadn't acknowledged having actually met Nina Palitov. Admittedly Rafe hadn't actually asked him if he had, but Michael certainly hadn't mentioned having met her, either. Not earlier, or when the two of them had spoken on the subject at Gabe's wedding; a conversation in which Michael also hadn't bothered to contradict Rafe when he had made the assumption that Nina Palitov was middle-aged.

'I saw the beautiful photographs, in the Sunday newspapers, of your younger brother's—Gabriel, is it?—wedding on Saturday. The three of you are very alike.'

Rafe had been studying the tips of his highly polished black shoes, but he now looked up at Nina Palitov, his eyes narrowing as he saw how the sun, shining in through the window behind him once again picked out those gold highlights in that glorious red hair, her eyes a soft moss-green against her creamy soft skin, and as for her lips…

Rafe cursed softly under his breath as he straightened before moving to sit back behind his desk, his already semi-hard erection having given an acknowledging throb in response to his looking appreciatively at Nina Palitov's lushly parted lips.

A totally unacceptable reaction as far as Rafe's intellect was concerned—he had always liked a lack of complication in those tall leggy blondes he was usually attracted to. They spent a few weeks of enjoying each other, mainly in bed, and with no expectations on either side. Nina Palitov, who she was, who her father was, made an attraction to her as complicated as hell.

Unfortunately his once again rapidly hardening manhood still seemed to have an entirely different opinion on the subject.

Rafe chose to ignore that physical reaction as he now looked across the width of his desk at Nina Palitov between narrowed lids. 'Yes, we are,' he bit out dismissively. 'And it was a lovely wedding. As lovely weddings go,' he added with a dismissive lack of interest.

Nina smiled at Rafe D'Angelo's obvious aversion to both weddings and marriage. 'I'm sure it isn't catching, like the measles or chickenpox!'

He gave a hard smile. 'I'm immune if it is!'

'Lucky you,' Nina came back lightly. 'Is that all you wished to discuss with me?'

Rafe D'Angelo blinked thick dark lashes, as if he had briefly forgotten that he was the one who had asked for this meeting, that emotion quickly masked as he gave a shrug. 'Not quite. Why don't you sit down for a few minutes?' he invited lightly, indicating the chair across from him, waiting until Nina was seated before continuing. 'Your father's security aside, I thought we should decide exactly what your role is going to be at Archangel for the period of the exhibition.'

Nina shrugged slender shoulders. 'As I've already stated, you will find that was already decided in the contract signed several weeks ago by my father, and your brother.'

'I've had a chance to read the contract in more detail now.' He nodded. 'And I really can't believe that you want to spend all of your time here for the next two weeks.'

'You can't?' Nina mused.

'No, I can't,' he repeated hardly. 'There's nothing more to do here now that the display cases have been delivered and put in place. I congratulate you on your work, by the way,' he seemed to add grudgingly. 'The display cases are exquisite.'

'Thank you,' she accepted shyly.

Nina had worked on making the display cases for almost four months now, since her father had first proposed the idea of exhibiting his jewellery collection in one of the New York galleries, taking several weeks and consultations with her father to decide on a combination of smooth pewter and bevelled glass, so as not to detract from the beauty of the jewels themselves. Each display case had its own intricate lock and security code, a code known only to Nina and her father. 'They will look even more impressive once the jewellery is inside them.'

'I'm sure.' Rafe D'Angelo nodded abruptly. 'The exhibition doesn't open until Saturday; surely it isn't going to take you more than a day or so to organise the display?'

'It's a very large collection.'

'Even so…'

Nina eyed him teasingly. 'If I didn't know better, Rafe, I would think that you were trying to get rid of me for at least three of those four days?'

And she would be right in thinking that, Rafe acknowledged with rising impatience. Damn it, he had the whole of Archangel to run, not just the Palitov Exhibition, and he didn't have the time—or the inclination—to cater to the whims and demands of the Palitov family. 'Not at all,' he dismissed smoothly.

'I spoke to my father on the telephone earlier, and he wishes me to extend his compliments to you, and invite you to his home for dinner this evening, if that's convenient?' the youngest member of the Palitov family invited formally.

The frown deepened on Rafe's brow at the invitation, knowing that Dmitri Palitov was as socially elusive as he was reclusive, but he now appeared to be inviting Rafe to go to his home for dinner this evening. Understandably so, perhaps, considering Rafe was now the D'Angelo brother in charge of the New York gallery the other man was entrusting his beloved jewellery collection to.

Rafe accepted all of that, he would just prefer not to become any more involved with the Palitov family than he already was, with Nina Palitov in particular. He especially didn't want the watchful Dmitri Palitov to witness Rafe's noticeably physical reaction to the man's daughter.

'Rafe?'

He scowled, his mouth firming. 'I have a previous engagement this evening, I'm afraid.' Thank heavens!

'I see.' Nina Palitov looked more than a little surprised at his refusal.

And no doubt that surprise was due to the fact that not too many people, if they were privileged enough to receive an invitation of any kind from the powerful Dmitri Palitov, would ever think of refusing it. As Rafe knew on a professional level he shouldn't refuse this dinner invitation either, but rather reorganise his date with the actress Jennifer Nichols for another evening instead. No doubt that was what Michael would expect him to do, but, as Rafe was feeling far from pleased with Michael at the moment, he really didn't give a damn what his big brother did or didn't think!

Nina knew that her father, for all that he had made the dinner invitation a request, would still be far from pleased that Rafe D'Angelo had refused that invitation.

At the same time as she, personally, couldn't help but admire Rafe for doing so. She loved her father dearly, but that didn't prevent her from being fully aware of the fact that his power made him far too accustomed to having his own way, to exerting his will on others, and expecting them to ask 'how high' when he said jump. Rafe D'Angelo obviously wasn't one of those people.

She nodded. 'My father suggested, if that should be the case, that you choose another evening convenient to yourself?'

'Let's see.' He made a point of opening and checking the large diary on his desk. 'Tomorrow evening seems to be free at the moment?'

'If that should change you can let me know tomorrow.' Nina nodded, still amused rather than concerned by Rafe's determination not to be dictated to by her father.

He raised dark brows. 'You still plan on coming in to the gallery every day?'

'My father expects it.'

Rafe D'Angelo relaxed back against his high-backed black leather chair as he looked at her through narrowed lids. 'And do you always do what your father expects?'

Nina stiffened at the taunting tone in his voice. 'It causes him less distress if I do, so yes,' she confirmed abruptly.

'Distress?' He quirked one dark and mocking brow.

'Yes.' Nina had no intention of elaborating on that explanation.

Her father's reasons for being so protective of her were none of Rafe D'Angelo's business. Or anyone else's, for that matter. It was what it was, and Nina accepted it as such. If she occasionally chafed against her father's need for that protection, then that was her own affair, and not Rafe D'Angelo's.

His golden, predatory gaze now raked over her with a deliberate, and mercilessly male, assessment, causing Nina's nipples to swell and firm as that gaze finally settled on the pertness of her breasts as they pressed snugly against her T-shirt. Nina drew her breath in softly as the cotton material acted as a mild abrasive against her bared flesh, deepening that arousal, at the same time as she felt a hot gush of dampness between her thighs.

Her body didn't seem to care that Rafe D'Angelo had deliberately set out to cause this response in her, that he was no doubt amusing himself at her expense as the ache in her nipples became an unbearable torture, and between her thighs swelled, became even more moist, as if in readiness for the stroke, the entry, of this man's touch.

But Nina cared. Her father's years of protection might have made her totally inadequate when it came to dealing with men as experienced as Rafe D'Angelo, but she wasn't about to let herself be the cause of any man's amusement, least of all the arrogant and mocking Rafe D'Angelo.

She stood up abruptly. 'I'll inform my father that you've accepted his dinner invitation for tomorrow evening,' she bit out abruptly.

Rafe raised his gaze reluctantly from enjoying the pertness of Nina Palitov's breasts, part of that enjoyment having been knowing, by the sudden tautness and swelling of her nipples, that she was far from immune to his appreciative gaze.

But one look at Nina's face, seeing the pained accusation in those moss-green eyes, the creamy pallor of her cheeks, and the defensive angle of her little pointed chin, and he felt like a complete heel for having behaved so badly. He was angry with his own unexpected physical response to this woman, with Michael for putting him in this position in the first place, even a little with Dmitri Palitov for the same reason, but that didn't give him the right to take that anger out on Nina.

Rafe stood up to move round to the side of his desk, the two of them now standing only inches apart. 'Will you be joining us for dinner tomorrow evening?' he prompted softly.

She looked up at him warily. 'I believe my father will expect me to be there to act as his hostess, yes.'

His brows rose. 'You don't live with your father?'

'Not quite.' Nina smiled slightly as she thought of her apartment. It was located in the same building that housed her father's penthouse apartment, a building that he also owned, and over which he had complete control of all security. Not the complete independence Nina would wish for, but it was better than she had inwardly expected after returning from Stanford.

Rafe D'Angelo eyed her quizzically. 'What does that mean?'

She gave a shake of her head; her father didn't discuss their living arrangements with anyone, and consequently some of that need for secrecy had rubbed off on her. 'It means I will be at my father's apartment for dinner tomorrow evening.'

'But you aren't about to tell me where you live?' Rafe D'Angelo guessed ruefully.

'No.'

'Not even if I were to offer to call for you and drive you to your father's apartment?'

'No,' she refused huskily. 'And I know my father intends to send one of his cars to collect you. He wanted me to confirm that your apartment is still on Fifth Avenue?'

Rafe felt a stirring of unease; Dmitri Palitov seemed to know far too much about him for comfort—far more than Rafe knew about the other man or his beautiful daughter.

'It is,' he confirmed slowly. 'Thank him for me, but I would prefer to drive myself.' Having his own transport meant that Rafe could leave when he'd had enough. He also bridled at the thought of being organised by the arrogant Dmitri Palitov!

Nina Palitov frowned at his refusal. 'I know my father would prefer to have one of his cars collect you.'

'And I would prefer to drive myself,' Rafe repeated unrelentingly.

'I very much doubt you know where he lives.'

'I doubt many people do,' he came back knowingly.

'No.'

He nodded briskly. 'Perhaps you would like to leave

the address with my secretary some time tomorrow? After you've spoken to your father again, of course.'

She chewed on her bottom lip, instantly drawing Rafe's attention to those pouting, slightly reddened lips, and in turn to those captivating moss-green eyes. He realised his mistake as he felt as if he were drowning in those smoky-green depths.

Just as he was aware the rest of him was being pulled, as if by a magnet, towards her, as his head slowly lowered—

'I should go and check security now,' Nina rasped abruptly even as she stepped back and away from him. 'I'll pass your message on to my father.'

'Fine.' Rafe straightened abruptly, inwardly cursing the obviously increasing attraction he felt towards Nina Palitov, and sincerely hoping his date this evening with Jennifer would put that attraction out of his mind—and appease his aching body! 'Do you want me to come down with you to view security in the basement?'

Nina gave a rueful smile at the obvious lack of enthusiasm in his voice. 'I believe that I can find my own way, thank you.'

Rafe eyed her irritably. 'I was being polite.'

'I noticed,' she drawled.

Rafe nodded abruptly before striding across to open the office door for her, a little disconcerted at instantly finding himself the focus of two pairs of wraparound sunglasses, the two bodyguards—Rich and Andy?—standing directly outside the door. 'I assure you, Miss Palitov has come to no harm while in my office,' he drawled mockingly.

There wasn't so much as an answering smile in either of those two grimly set faces, neither man sparing Rafe a second glance as Nina stepped out into the hallway. 'Good day to you, Mr D'Angelo,' she murmured before walking off towards the lift, the two men falling into step behind her.

Which in no way hindered Rafe of the view of Nina Palitov's heart-shaped backside in those tight-fitting denims. A view his once-again throbbing body enjoyed to the full.

He was in trouble—serious trouble!—Rafe acknowledged with a low groan, if just looking at the perfect curve of Nina's bottom in a pair of tight-fitting denims could succeed in making his shaft swell and ache!

CHAPTER THREE

'You like this Raphael D'Angelo who is coming to dine with us this evening?'

Nina tensed, her hand shaking slightly, as she paused in pouring her father's usual pre-dinner drink of single malt whisky from the cut-glass decanter into one of the matching glasses on the silver salver. She waited several seconds for her hand to stop shaking, and to compose her expression, before she finished pouring, and then turned to carry the glass over to her father. 'Have I told you how handsome you look this evening, Papa?' she complimented lightly.

'A man of almost seventy-nine cannot be called handsome,' he drawled dismissively, his English still accented, despite his having lived in the States for more than half his life. 'Distinguished, perhaps. But I am too far beyond the flush of youth to ever be called handsome.'

'You always look handsome to me, Papa,' Nina assured him warmly.

Because he did. Her father might be heading towards his eightieth year, but his habitual air of suppressed vitality made him seem much younger, and his iron-grey hair was still thick and plentiful, his face one of chiselled strength, even if his eyes had faded over the years to a pale green rather than the same moss-green as her own.

Her father gave her a knowing look. 'You are avoiding answering my original question.'

That was probably because Nina had no idea what had prompted her father to ask it.

She had once again spent the day at the gallery, organising the final arrangement of the display cabinets. She'd felt slightly on edge in case she should see Rafe D'Angelo again, and then a certain amount of disappointment when she'd left the gallery at four o'clock without catching so much as a glimpse of its charismatic owner.

A disappointment she had chastised herself for feeling as she lay soaking in a perfumed bath an hour or so later; Rafe D'Angelo was not a man she should become in the least interested in. He was arrogant, mocking, and, even more importantly, not in the least bit interested in her.

Even so, Nina hadn't been able to resist switching on her laptop and looking him up on the Internet once she had finished her bath, sitting on her bed in her dressing gown, her wet hair wrapped in a towel, to scroll through the pages and pages of information and gossip on the highly photographed Raphael D'Angelo. She'd told herself that it was because she needed to know all that she could about the man her father had invited to dinner this evening—other than the fact that he brought out a physical reaction in her that she found distinctly uncomfortable.

It had taken her several minutes of scrolling before she found a photograph of him from the previous evening, as he enjoyed an intimate dinner for two at an exclusive New York restaurant, with the beautiful actress Jennifer Nichols—obviously the 'previous engagement' that had prompted him to refuse her father's initial dinner invitation. Nina had switched off her laptop in disgust.

Nina had decided that Rafe D'Angelo was nothing

more than a rake and a womaniser, and she refused to waste any more of her time—or her emotions—on him.

'You are still avoiding it, Nina,' her father prompted gently.

She gave a rueful shake of her head. 'That's probably because I have no idea what prompted you to ask such a question, Papa.'

'You are looking very beautiful this evening, *maya doch*.'

'Are you saying I don't normally?' she teased.

Her father gave an answering smile. 'You know you are always beautiful to me, Nina. But tonight you seem to have made a special effort to be so.'

Probably because, after seeing that photograph of Rafe D'Angelo with the actress Jennifer Nichols, that was exactly what she had done! Which was pretty silly of her; she could never hope to compete with the beauty or sophistication of the A-list actress.

Nor should she want to.

Rafe D'Angelo meant nothing to her. As she meant nothing to him.

'And I do not believe you have made this special effort on my behalf,' her father added softly. 'So, do you like this Raphael D'Angelo?' he persisted.

Nina gave an exasperated sigh. 'I don't know him well enough to like or dislike him, Papa.'

'You spent some time alone with him yesterday.'

She gave a pained frown. 'I thought we had agreed, after I left Stanford, that I would continue to have my own security detail but that they would only report to you if I was in any danger?'

'We did,' her father confirmed unconcernedly. 'And that has not changed, nor will it. I did not receive this information from your own security detail, Nina. I do not need to do so, when I have my own,' he added softly.

'Let me guess, one of the workmen who accompanied me to the gallery yesterday was one of your men,' she guessed impatiently. 'Papa, you really shouldn't have done that.' She sighed.

He shrugged. 'I am merely interested to know what you and D'Angelo talked about for the twenty-three minutes you were alone with him in his office,' he prompted lightly.

'Twenty-three minutes?' Nina repeated, incredulous. 'You timed how long I was in there?'

'My man did, yes,' her father dismissed unconcernedly. 'Are you aware of D'Angelo's reputation with women?'

'Papa, I'm not going to discuss this with you any further!' She threw her hands up in the air in disgust. 'My meeting yesterday with Rafe D'Angelo was purely business.'

'Rafe?'

She nodded. 'It's what he prefers to be called. And my meeting with him yesterday was on your behalf, I might add.' She felt a blush warm in her cheeks as she remembered those few seconds, just prior to her leaving Rafe's office, when it had almost felt as if he had been about to kiss her. Before, because of her own nervousness, she had put an end to that intimacy.

'I do not want to see you hurt by this man, *maya doch*,' her father said gently.

'And I'm assuring you that isn't going to happen,' Nina insisted firmly. 'I told you, I haven't even decided yet whether or not I even like Raphael D'Angelo!'

'That's a pity, because I've decided I like you, Nina,' drawled an infuriatingly familiar voice.

Nina felt the colour drain from her cheeks as she turned sharply to face Rafe D'Angelo as he stood in the doorway slightly behind her father's butler, obviously having just arrived, and looking breathtakingly handsome in his black evening clothes, with that overlong ebony hair brushed back from his handsome face.

Rafe almost laughed out loud at the look of dismay on Nina Palitov's face as she realised he had overheard her telling remark in regard to him.

But he only almost laughed…

Not only was it not particularly amusing to hear her state her uncertainty of liking him so plainly, but the way she looked this evening had totally robbed him of the breath to laugh even if he had wanted to!

Nina was wearing a gown the same moss-green as her eyes, a knee-length sheath of a gown that clung lovingly to her womanly curves, with two ribbon straps across her otherwise bare shoulders and arms, the swell of her breasts visible above the low neckline, those long legs revealed as being slender and shapely, with three-inch-heeled shoes of the same colour as her gown bringing her height up to six feet. Her fiery red hair, that crowning glory, was held back from her temples with two diamond clips, but otherwise fell in that tumbling cascade of curls down the length of her spine to rest above the shapely bottom he had so enjoyed looking at yesterday as she'd walked away from him.

'Mr D'Angelo, sir.' The English butler maintained a wooden expression as he belatedly announced Rafe's arrival.

'Do come in and join us, Mr D'Angelo,' his host invited smoothly.

Rafe gave the butler a ruefully sympathetic smile as he stepped past him into the sitting room, that smile freezing, becoming fixed, as he looked at his host fully for the first time and realised that Dmitri Palitov was sitting in a wheelchair rather than one of the cream velvet armchairs!

'I trust you will understand why I do not get up to greet you, Mr D'Angelo,' Dmitri Palitov drawled dryly as he obviously saw Rafe's look of surprise.

A surprise Rafe quickly masked beneath a politely bland smile as he strode across the room to shake the hand the older man held out to him. 'No problem. And please call me Rafe,' he invited lightly as he released his hand from the other man's strong grip. 'Despite being unsure as to whether or not she likes me, your daughter already calls me Rafe,' he added softly before glancing challengingly across to where Nina stood silently watching the two men. His glance was slightly censorious, but not because of what Nina had said; Rafe would have appreciated a heads up in regard to knowing her father was in a wheelchair before actually meeting his host this evening.

Although he acknowledged that might have been a little difficult for her to do. Nina had done as he'd asked, and left her father's address with his assistant earlier, but Rafe admitted to going out of his way to ensure the two of them didn't actually meet during the hours she had been at the gallery today.

Because he was annoyed.

With himself, not Nina.

Nina could have no idea that his evening with Jennifer Nichols had gone so disastrously wrong for the simple reason he couldn't stop thinking about Nina. Or, at least, his rebellious body had refused to stop thinking about Nina.

So much so that Rafe hadn't felt an ounce of desire to bed the beautiful actress at the end of the evening, and had instead merely kissed Jennifer on the cheek after driving her home, before then going home alone to his own apartment and his empty bed. Not to go straight to sleep, unfortunately, as a certain part of his anatomy had refused to comply, and even when he had finally slept it had been fitfully, and filled with dreams of bedding flame-haired Nina!

Consequently Rafe hadn't been in the best of moods all day; he'd certainly felt no inclination to actually see or talk to the woman who was causing his present lack of sexual desire to bed another woman. Something that had never happened to him before, and Rafe didn't appreciate that it was happening to him now either.

'Do not blame Nina for her earlier remark,' his host advised ruefully. 'What you overheard her say was merely as a result of my having just teased her.'

Rafe wondered exactly what Dmitri Palitov had been teasing his daughter about to have elicited such a vehement response from her, and that curiosity was added to by the sudden blush that now coloured Nina's cheeks.

'Would you care to join me in a glass of whisky before dinner, Rafe?' his host offered politely.

'Thank you, Dmitri.' Rafe nodded, watching through narrowed lids as Nina silently crossed the room to the array of drinks on the sideboard, that red hair like a living flame as it tumbled down the length of her spine as she kept her back turned towards them while she poured his whisky.

'I trust your previous engagement, yesterday evening, was successful, Rafe?'

Rafe turned back as his host spoke to him once again, knowing by the hardness of the older man's expression that Dmitri Palitov had noticed his interest in his daughter, and wasn't sure as to whether he approved or not.

As the other man was also aware of exactly what—and with whom—Rafe's previous engagement had been last night?

The mockery in those pale green eyes looking so challengingly up into his indicated the answer to that question was a resounding yes. Dmitri Palitov knew exactly where and with whom Rafe had been the previous evening.

'Really, Papa,' Nina drawled mockingly as she crossed the room to hand Rafe his glass of whisky, her hand deliberately not coming into contact with his as she did so. 'We really shouldn't embarrass Rafe by enquiring as to whether or not he enjoyed his evening with Miss Nichols.'

Great; not only did Dmitri Palitov know who Rafe had spent the previous evening with, but it appeared Nina was aware of it too. And the mockery in her expression as she looked at him from beneath thick dark lashes indicated she had drawn her own conclusions about how that evening had ended too.

Nina felt a certain amount of satisfaction in seeing the look of discomfort on Rafe D'Angelo's face as he realised both she and her father were aware he had considered an evening—and night?—spent with the beautiful actress to be more pressing than accepting a dinner invitation from an important client of one of the galleries he owned with his two brothers.

'Not at all,' he finally answered tautly. 'And I had a very pleasant evening, thank you.'

Her father chuckled softly. 'Not much escapes the attention of the press nowadays, Rafe; it is the price one pays when one is in the public eye.'

'Obviously.' He scowled as he took a swallow of the whisky in his glass.

Nina felt a certain admiration for the fact that Rafe made no attempt to try and excuse his behaviour; many men, when confronted by a man as powerful as her father, would have tried to bluster their way out of the situation. Obviously, Rafe D'Angelo had no intention of apologising to any man, or woman, for what he did or didn't choose to do.

'Perhaps you would care to see the jewellery collection before dinner, Rafe?' her father offered lightly.

'I would like that very much, thank you,' the younger man accepted.

Nina accompanied the two men to her father's private sanctuary, impressed as Rafe proceeded to murmur both suitable admiration and knowledge of the beautiful jewellery her father had collected over the years.

It really was a truly amazing and unique collection with dozens and dozens of priceless pieces of jewellery; several necklaces, bracelets and rings had once been owned by the Tsarina Alexandra herself. But every single piece of that magnificent collection had a history of its own, and her father had spent years learning every single one of those histories.

The mood for the evening was much more relaxed once they returned to the sitting room, the conversation over dinner lightly interesting as they all first discussed the exhibition to take place next week, before the conversation moved on to politics, and the inevitable subject of sport, most specifically American Football, as the two men lingered over their brandy and cigars.

Nina had contributed to the first three subjects, but American Football just made her want to yawn.

A reaction that made Rafe D'Angelo smile as he caught her in the obvious act of trying to stifle one of those yawns.

'I believe we're boring Nina, Dmitri,' he drawled teas-

ingly, obviously far more relaxed now than he had been
when he'd first arrived.

'*Doch*?' Her father looked at her enquiringly.

'I'm a little tired, that's all,' Nina assured with a smile.

'It's late.' Rafe nodded. 'Time I was leaving.'

'Please don't go on my account,' Nina protested awk-
wardly. 'It's been a busy week, that's all.'

'No, I really should go now. I have work in the morning,' he assured dismissively. 'Perhaps I could escort you
home, Nina?' he added huskily.

She felt her heart beat faster, louder, at the thought
of having the rakishly handsome Rafe D'Angelo escort
her to her door, perhaps to even have him kiss her goodnight—

Obviously she had drunk far too much of her father's
excellent wine with her meal, because Rafe hadn't so
much as hinted this evening, by word or deed, that he was
in the least interested in kissing her goodnight!

No, his offer to escort her home had obviously been
made out of politeness, and possibly even as a sop to her
father's obviously old-fashioned manners.

'That is very gentlemanly of you, Rafe.' Surprisingly
her father was the one to answer the other man before
Nina had a chance to do so.

'My daughter has become far too independent, after
her years at university, for my liking.'

Rafe saw the flash of irritation in Nina's eyes before
it was quickly masked. As evidence that she didn't particularly enjoy, or want, to have those bodyguards following her about day, and possibly night, too? He would
well imagine it could feel extremely stifling, as well as
being a complete downer on her personal life.

Which posed the question, did Nina have a man in that
personal life? Rafe would imagine it would take a very

determined man to date the daughter of Dmitri Palitov, let alone put up with the oppressive presence of those bodyguards every time the two of them went out together. And as for moving on to anything more intimate, well, it must be a logistical, and emotional, nightmare!

It also begged the question as to why Nina put up with it. She was a beautiful woman in her mid-twenties, obviously intelligent to have obtained a degree from Stanford, and her comments during the conversation this evening had been both learned and considered. She was also well qualified, and possessed a true talent for design, if those beautiful display cases in the east gallery at Archangel were an indication of her work, so why did she continue to allow her father to limit and watch her movements in the obsessive way that he did?

Another part of the unanswered mystery that Nina Palitov was fast becoming to him...

A mystery, the more time he spent in her company, Rafe found he wanted answers to.

'Nina?' he prompted huskily as he moved to stand behind her chair in preparation for leaving.

'Fine,' she bit out tensely. 'I have no objection to your coming down to the next floor in the lift with me, and walking me to my apartment door, if that's what you want to do.'

Rafe raised his brows. 'You live in this building?'

'Yes.' Her eyes glittered bright with challenge as she looked up at him.

Well, that certainly explained her comment yesterday when Rafe had asked if she lived with her father.

'I see,' he said slowly.

Her mouth tightened. 'Somehow I doubt that very much.'

'Nina,' her father put in reprovingly at the sharpness of her tone.

She closed her eyes briefly, drawing in two calming breaths before opening them again, her smile now one of stiff politeness. 'Thank you, Rafe, I would appreciate your walking me to my door,' she said tightly as he held her chair back for her to stand up, before she moved round the table to kiss her father warmly on the cheek. 'I will see you tomorrow, Papa.' Her voice softened noticeably.

'As always, *maya doch*.' He touched her cheek affectionately before turning to Rafe. 'It has been a pleasure to meet and talk with you this evening, Rafe,' he added formally.

'You too, sir.' Rafe nodded distractedly, his concerned gaze fixed on Nina as she swept from the dining room without so much as a second glance at either man.

'My jewellery collection is very precious to me, Rafe.' Dmitri Palitov spoke quietly beside him.

Rafe turned to look at the older man. 'It's very impressive,' he acknowledged slowly, uncertain as to where this change of subject was going.

'Each piece is priceless.' Dmitri nodded. 'But, beautiful as my collection is, valuable as it is, I value my daughter far above any rubies or diamonds.'

Ah...

'As such,' the older man continued hardly, 'I will always do anything and everything within my power to ensure her health and happiness.'

'Understandably,' Rafe answered non-committally.

'Yes?' Dmitri Palitov spoke with that same hard challenge.

It was the first time that Rafe had ever been warned off a woman by her father, but, yes, he believed he understood this for exactly what it was.

'Nina is a big girl now, Dmitri.' He spoke evenly.

'Yes, she is.' The older man nodded. 'But even so, perhaps you should know that I will not look kindly on any man who chooses to hurt my daughter. Whether it be intentionally or unintentionally.' Those green eyes, so like his daughter's, glittered in warning.

Pretty succinct and to the point—and unmistakably Dmitri Palitov's way of warning him off.

'Thank you for an enjoyable evening, sir.' Rafe held his hand out formally to the other man.

'D'Angelo.' Dmitri Palitov shook that hand briefly, those green eyes pale and hard as some of the jewels in this man's private collection.

Nina wondered if Rafe found the silence between the two of them as uncomfortable as she did as they stepped into the private lift together minutes later. Probably not. His offer to escort her to her apartment had been a politeness, nothing more, and one that she knew would soon be over as the lift halted on the lower floor just seconds later.

'You don't have your bodyguards with you this evening?' he prompted coolly as he walked beside her to her apartment, the heels of her shoes clicking on the marble floor in the otherwise silent hallway.

She gave a tight, humourless smile. 'Even my father accepts that I have no need for them here. He owns the whole building, controls all security, and no one is allowed in or out of the building without his approval,' she explained dismissively as Rafe eyed her questioningly.

He frowned darkly. 'Isn't that taking the protective-father role a bit far?'

'Possibly,' she accepted tightly.

'Why the hell do you put up with it?' he bit out impatiently.

Her mouth tightened. 'I don't believe that's any of your business.'

Rafe scowled his frustration with that reply. 'How long has your father been in a wheelchair?'

Nina flicked him a surprised glance. 'Almost twenty years.'

Rafe nodded. 'And you don't think it might have been a good idea to have told me that before I met him this evening?'

'I don't quite see… It didn't even occur to me. Or your brother, obviously,' she dismissed impatiently. 'I grew up seeing my father in a wheelchair. I don't even notice he's in one now.'

No, of course she didn't, Rafe acknowledged ruefully, and she was right, Michael hadn't thought to pre-warn him either. Yet another thing about the Palitov family that his big brother had forgotten to mention.

'How did it happen?' Rafe prompted softly.

'I— An accident,' she answered stiffly.

Rafe's eyes narrowed. 'What sort of accident?'

'A car accident.' She frowned. 'His spine was severed, and he's been confined to a wheelchair ever since, end of story.' She used her key card to open the door to her apartment. 'Thank you for—'

'Invite me in, Nina!'

Nina looked up quickly, her eyes wide as she saw the intensity of Rafe's expression; those golden eyes glittered down at her, a nerve pulsing in his tightly clenched jaw. 'I— No, I don't think that would be a good idea.'

'Because your father wouldn't approve?' he came back derisively.

She bristled. 'My refusal has nothing to do with my father.' And everything to do with the fact that Nina had been totally physically aware of this man all evening, in a way she could never remember being aware of any other man. Nina had no explanation for it, she just knew that she was drawn to him like a moth to a flame—and probably with the same results; she would get seriously burnt if she gave in to that attraction.

'Oh, I think it has everything to do with him.' Rafe eyed her mockingly.

Nina gave a pained frown. 'You don't understand.'

'You're right, I don't.' Rafe gave an impatient shake of his head. 'I don't understand why a vibrantly beautiful and talented young woman would allow her life to be dictated to by her overbearing father.'

'My father is not—' She broke off, breathing deeply. 'As I said, you can't possibly understand.'

'Then invite me in for coffee and explain it to me.' Rafe raised his hands and placed them either side of her on the doorframe as he leant into her.

She blinked at his sudden proximity, her heart pounding loudly in her chest as she looked up at him searchingly, shaking her head when she found herself unable to read anything from the intensity of his expression. 'You already had coffee in my father's apartment.'

'For the love of—! Will you just invite me into your apartment, Nina?' he ground out harshly.

Her mouth had gone dry, her throat moving as she attempted to swallow past that dryness before answering him. 'I said I don't think that's a good idea.' It was a very bad idea, when Nina was aware of everything about Rafe, from his overlong dark hair, muscled shoulders, flat abdomen, and long, long legs...

'Probably not,' he grated unapologetically. 'But ask me in anyway.'

Nina gave him a puzzled look. 'What's this all about, Rafe?'

He gave a humourless smile. 'One way or another, it's been one hell of an evening. When I arrived I overheard my hostess saying she doesn't like me.'

'That I wasn't sure I liked you,' she corrected, colour warming her cheeks. 'And my father explained the reason why.'

'Partly, yes. An interesting man, your father,' he added harshly. 'The perfect host, so gracious and charming.'

She blinked. 'Why do you sound so mocking when you say that?'

'Probably because I was just very politely but unmistakably warned off by your father,' he rasped exasperatedly.

'I don't understand.' Nina gave a puzzled shake of her head; the two men had seemed to get on well enough during dinner. 'Warned off from what?'

'You.' Rafe glowered down at her.

Her eyes widened. 'Me?'

He nodded grimly. 'Your father took the opportunity, after you had left the dining room just now, to oh-so-subtly warn me that he would prefer it if I stayed well away from his daughter in future.'

'Oh, no.' She felt her face pale, as she knew her father was perfectly capable of doing exactly that.

And for once in her life she resented her father's overprotective attitude. For once in her life she wanted what she wanted. And tonight, watching Rafe surreptitiously all evening, becoming more and more attracted to him by the moment, had revealed to her that she wanted Rafe D'Angelo.

'Yes,' Rafe confirmed hardly. 'Does he do that to every man you come into contact with, or did he just single me out for special attention?'

'I have no idea.' But she intended finding out, intended

having a heart-to-heart conversation with her father first thing tomorrow morning. 'I'll speak to him— He really did that?' She winced.

'He really did, yes,' Rafe confirmed harshly.

'In that case I apologise.' She frowned. 'I have no idea why my father would even think that you— Why he would think there was any possibility of the two of us ever—' She broke off, realising she was just making this situation worse than it already was. If that was possible.

How could her father have done such a thing? How could he have humiliated her in that way, and with a man she might possibly have reason to see on a daily basis for the next two weeks, at least? A man she felt drawn to as if by a magnet.

'Invite me in, please, Nina,' Rafe pressed huskily.

She looked up at him uncertainly, the pulse beating wildly in her throat as she heard the unmistakable husky intensity in his voice and saw the glitter had deepened in those golden eyes.

'I— Why are you so determined I should be the one to invite you into my apartment?' Her acquaintance with this man so far hadn't given her the impression Rafe was a man who waited for an invitation before doing just as he pleased. 'You aren't a vampire, or something, are you?' she added lightly, in an effort to alleviate some of the sexual tension that swirled and swelled around them.

'Hardly.' He gave a humourless smile. 'Although I have been known to bite a neck or two!'

Nina instantly regretted her teasing. 'Why are you so set on my inviting you into my apartment, Rafe?' she repeated determinedly, tempted, oh-so-tempted, by both Rafe and the idea of, for once in her life, thwarting both her father and her bodyguards.

His mouth firmed. 'Because I don't think you need another bossy and dominating man telling you what to do.'

Her cheeks paled. 'My father is— He has his reasons for behaving in the way that he— You don't understand,' she repeated softly.

'You're right, I don't,' Rafe rasped grimly. 'I don't understand why any beautiful and intelligent woman would allow her father to dictate the terms under which she conducts her life!'

How could he? How could anyone understand the fear her father had lived with on a daily basis for the past twenty years, the dread that Nina might one day be taken from him?

As his beloved wife had been so cruelly taken from him.

CHAPTER FOUR

'INVITE ME IN, Nina,' Rafe encouraged gruffly as he saw the indecision in her expression.

She looked up at him wordlessly for several long seconds, before nodding abruptly and turning on her heel to enter the shadowed hallway of her apartment, turning on the soft glow of the overhead light as she did so.

Rafe prowled in after Nina before closing the door gently behind him, his gaze intent on hers as he took her slowly into his arms to mould her curves against his. Her hands moved instinctively to his shoulders as she raised her startled gaze searchingly to his, obviously totally aware of the fullness of his arousal pressing against the softness of her abdomen—that same arousal that had been missing the evening before with Jennifer Nichols.

'There's just no way for a man to hide his reaction to a beautiful woman, is there?' he murmured self-derisively.

Her silky throat moved as she swallowed before speaking. 'I— No, I guess not.'

Rafe's gaze was fixed on her lushly pouting lips. Those same lips that had been driving him insane all evening, when he had been unable to drag his gaze away from watching Nina part them as she sipped her wine, or put food in her mouth, almost groaning out loud when she flicked her tongue across those lips to capture the morsel of lemon mousse that had smeared her bottom lip as she'd eaten her dessert.

Perhaps he had deserved Dmitri Palitov's earlier warning, after all, regarding Nina. No doubt the older man had made a note of every single occasion Rafe had been unable to stop imagining all the ways Nina's lushly provocative lips might give a man pleasure.

She moistened those lips with the tip of her tongue now. 'I— Do you want coffee?'

'No.'

'Oh.'

Rafe could sense Nina's nervousness, just as he could feel the trembling of her body curved so intimately into and against his. He felt the warmth of her hands through the material of his jacket and shirt. Long and elegantly tapered hands that he had ached all evening to press against his bared and throbbing flesh.

Yes, maybe he had fully deserved Dmitri Palitov's warning where Nina was concerned.

There was no way Nina could possibly miss the fierceness of the hunger that now lit Rafe's eyes to a molten, heated gold before his gaze lowered to the swell of her breasts visible above the low neckline of her gown.

'I want to kiss you, Nina,' he groaned harshly.

'Yes,' she groaned, leaning weakly against him as her legs trembled and her hands tightened on his muscled shoulders.

'And then I would like to bare and caress these pretty breasts.' Both his hands moved up to cup beneath their fullness, the soft sweep of the pad of his thumb unerringly finding the swollen tip.

'With my tongue and teeth as well as—'

'Will you stop talking about it, Rafe, and just do it?' Nina groaned softly, almost panting she was so aroused.

Her teeth clenched as she felt that arousal sweep down and through her body, a rush of dampness moistening the already swollen and aching folds between her thighs.

'You aren't afraid to take what you want, after all.' He gave a throaty and appreciative chuckle as he lifted one of his hands and entwined it in the fiery length of her hair, looking deeply into her eyes for several searching seconds before using that pressure to tilt her head back and sideways as he claimed her lips with his own.

Firm and yet softly sensual lips, that sipped and tasted hers for long torturous minutes, his tongue a fiery caress against that melting softness before his kiss hardened, deepened, as his tongue plunged into the heated warmth of her mouth, duelling before entwining sensuously with hers.

Nina's hands moved across Rafe's shoulders to allow her fingers to become entangled in the silky length of his ebony hair as she held him against her. He continued to kiss her deeply, hungrily, his hands moving restlessly down the length of her spine before cupping her bottom and pulling her into the hardness of his arousal, leaving Nina in no doubt as to the length and thickness of that arousal as his shaft throbbed and pulsed against her thighs.

That continued sensual assault, of Rafe's lips and tongue, drove Nina's arousal higher still, until her whole body felt on fire with the need for more. So much more.

She gasped for air, her throat arching as Rafe's mouth released hers to seek out the hollows and dips of her neck. One of Rafe's hand's moved to slip the thin shoulder strap of her gown down onto her arm as the heat of his lips now seared across her exposed skin. The zip of Nina's gown felt cold against her heated flesh as he slid the fastening slowly downwards and allowed both straps of her gown to fall the length of her arms and expose her naked breasts.

The heat of Rafe's lips now followed the slope of her bared breasts, his tongue licking, tasting, tormenting her fevered flesh. Nina's knees buckled, only the strength of Rafe's arm about her waist continuing to hold her up as she felt the heat of his mouth close over the swollen aching tip of her breast before he suckled it deeply into that heat.

Oh, dear heaven!

And it was heaven, dear, sweet torturous heaven, as Rafe's hand cupped, caressed that aching nipple as he turned his attention to her other breast, suckling that swollen nipple deeply and then softly, his fingers and tongue a never-ending torment against her roused and sensitive flesh, pleasuring her, and causing those folds to swell between her thighs as her juices first dampened and then completely wet her panties.

Nina gave a choked sob. She was on fire; she needed— oh, God—she *needed—*

She gasped her disappointment as Rafe's mouth released her and he raised his head slightly, eyes dark as he gazed down at the red and swollen tips of her breasts.

'So pretty,' he murmured gruffly as he touched each of her swollen nipples in turn with the softness of his fingertips.

Nina could barely breathe as she waited to see what Rafe intended to do next. Hoping it was what she wanted him to do.

Rafe gazed his fill of Nina's beautiful breasts, tipped by pretty peach nipples that had become red and engorged from the attention of his hands and mouth. Nipples that still begged for those attentions.

Attention he was more than willing to give her. Just as

he longed to explore the silken folds between her thighs. He could smell Nina's arousal now, creamy and yet with an added enticing spice. And he longed to lap up that creaminess, to drink in her essence even as his lips and tongue explored those swollen folds, and then he wanted to swallow her down, to be able to taste her in his mouth and throat for hours afterwards.

That Nina wanted those things too he was in no doubt as she looked up at him, green eyes dark with her arousal, a flush to her creamy cheeks, and her lips parted invitingly as she breathed raggedly.

And he couldn't do it.

Oh, Rafe knew what the newspapers printed about him—almost on a daily basis when he was in New York, it seemed! That he had a parade of beautiful women passing through his bedroom, women he changed as often as he did his silk bed sheets. And up to a point that was true. There had never been a shortage of women whose bed he might share, for a night or, indeed, several nights or weeks.

Even so, Rafe had his own set of rules when it came to the women who briefly entered his life. He never offered false promises. He never cheated on the woman he was currently sleeping with. And when it stopped being fun, for either of them, he gently brought that relationship to an end.

Nina wasn't like any other woman Rafe had ever known. She was more. So much more. And emotionally complicated, in a way Rafe had always chosen to avoid in the past.

She was much younger than those other women for one thing, had spent all of her twenty-four years sheltered by her overprotective father, and so lacked both the sophistication and cynicism that had allowed those other women to accept the few weeks of a relationship Rafe had to offer them.

There was also the fact, ridiculous as it might seem in the current circumstances, that he was here this evening at the invitation of Nina's father, a man as dangerous as he was powerful, and with whom Rafe's gallery was currently doing business. Rafe had never mixed business with pleasure.

And lastly, even more ridiculously, he and Nina hadn't so much as been out on a date together yet.

'Rafe?' Nina questioned uncertainly as he stood silent and unmoving in front of her, his face set in grim lines as he looked down at her. She felt totally exposed with her gown down about her waist, her breasts still bared, swollen and aching from the touch of his lips and hands.

His jaw was tightly clenched, dark lashes shielding the expression in his eyes as he reached down to pull the straps of her gown back up her arms and into place on her shoulders. Nina was too taken aback by his actions to offer the least resistance when Rafe turned her away from him slightly so that he could refasten the zip up the length of her spine.

Telling her more clearly than any words that this encounter was over.

'Have dinner with me tomorrow evening, Nina?'

She turned sharply back to face him, looking up at him searchingly, but was unable to read anything from the grimness of his expression. 'Why?' she finally breathed.

His brows rose. 'Do you usually ask why when a man invites you out to dinner with him?'

Nina's chin tilted defensively. 'Only when that same man went out to dinner with another woman the previous evening.'

His mouth tightened. 'I have no intention of seeing Jennifer Nichols again.'

'Does she know that?'

'Oh, yes.' His mouth twisted derisively.

She gave a shake of her head. 'I— Our lovemaking just now was—it was…an aberration, Rafe, for both of us, probably.' Although she wasn't sure it could be called 'our' lovemaking, when she had been the one half undressed and Rafe had remained as immaculately clothed as he had been when he first arrived this evening.

Well, perhaps not quite so immaculately. His hair was more than a little tousled from having her fingers running through it, and there was a smear of her peach lip gloss at the corner of Rafe's mouth.

'Don't feel you have to invite me out to dinner because things got a little out of hand just now,' she added firmly.

'An aberration?' Rafe repeated ruefully as he fought back the urge to chuckle.

Which, considering the circumstances, was again more than a little unexpected!

Rafe had been rendered breathless by Nina's appearance when he'd arrived for dinner earlier this evening. He had spent several hours over that dinner politely but nevertheless verbally fencing with her father while unable to take his eyes off Nina, only for Dmitri Palitov to take off the gloves completely at the end of the evening and issue him an outright warning in regard to Rafe staying away from his daughter.

The latter had annoyed Rafe intensely, so much so that he had intended to just walk Nina back to her apartment and then leave, before congratulating himself on being well rid of all of the Palitov family. Apart from their business connection, of course. An intent that had disappeared the moment they had arrived outside Nina's apartment and Rafe had realised he wasn't ready to say goodnight to her quite yet.

'Yes, an aberration,' she insisted firmly. 'I want you to know I'm certainly not in the habit of allowing random men to make love to me.'

'"Random men"?' Rafe couldn't hold back his amused chuckle this time. 'Is that how you think of me, Nina, as just some random man you happened to make love with?'

She frowned her irritation at his humour. 'I obviously drank far too much wine with my dinner.'

'And I believe you're being deliberately insulting now, Nina,' Rafe drawled knowingly.

Yes, she was, Nina acknowledged heavily. Because there was no way she could explain her wanton behaviour just now to Rafe, of all people. To do so would be to admit that he had got under her skin, past her guard, and made her long for things, for the freedom to give in totally to this attraction.

'Maybe,' she allowed tightly. 'But I would like you to leave now.'

'And do you always get what you want?'

Hardly ever, Nina acknowledged ruefully.

Oh, materially she could have anything she wanted; her father's wealth had always ensured that. But she'd had such dreams and plans for her future when she'd returned home from Stanford three years ago, clutching her degree proudly in her hands. Of starting up her own design business. Of making a success of that business. Of meeting a man she could love, and who would love her. Of marrying and one day having a family of her own.

And instead she had been sucked straight back into her father's reclusive and overprotective lifestyle.

No, that was unfair to her father; she was the one who had allowed herself to be sucked straight back into her father's life of bodyguards, who hadn't fought hard enough for the things she wanted for herself.

Because her father had looked so much frailer than when she had left him three years earlier. Because he had obviously needed to have her close to him again and know she was safe. So Nina had put her own dreams and hopes on hold, so much so she had all but forgotten about them until now.

Until Rafe D'Angelo and this attraction she felt towards him had forced her to remember them.

'Nina?' Rafe prompted softly at her continued silence.

She gave a deep sigh. 'Thank you for your dinner invitation, Rafe, but I would rather not.'

'Why not?'

She eyed him irritably. 'Do you usually ask a woman that when she says no to you?'

Those chiselled lips curved up into a smile as she turned his earlier remark back on him. 'That's a little difficult to say, when I can't remember it ever having happened before.'

Nina frowned. 'Well, it's happening now.'

The smile slowly disappeared as he looked down at her searchingly. 'But for all the wrong reasons,' he finally murmured softly.

Her eyes flashed in warning. 'Don't pretend to know the first thing about me, Rafe!'

He shrugged. 'Deny if you can that it's just easier, because of your father, if you refuse to go out with me.'

It was easier. Not only that, Nina knew it was the right thing to do. Except she wanted to accept. This attraction she felt for Rafe made her want to rebel against the limitations her father had imposed on her life.

'And what are your reasons for asking, Rafe?' she asked cautiously. 'Are you asking me out to dinner because you like me, and want to spend time with me? Or are you asking me out to dinner because you're annoyed with my father, because of his warning earlier, and you just want to annoy him back?'

'That isn't very flattering, Nina. To you or to me,' Rafe drawled huskily.

She shrugged. 'Not if the latter is true, no.'

Rafe eyed her thoughtfully, not sure if he felt more irritated by Nina's suspicions regarding his dinner invitation, or by the reality of the life she must have led to make her draw those conclusions in the first place. Either way, he had no intention of backing off. 'It isn't,' he bit out economically. 'So, is your answer to be yes or no, Nina?'

The indecision in those beautiful moss-green eyes made Rafe want to put further pressure on her, to goad or seduce her, whichever worked, into accepting his dinner invitation. But he held back from doing either of those things. It had to be Nina's decision; he had meant it when he told her earlier that he considered one dominating man in her life telling her what to do as being more than enough for any woman.

And so he remained silent, inwardly willing Nina to accept his dinner invitation, at the same time as he questioned himself as to when it had become so important to him that she did.

Maybe when her beauty had rendered him breathless when he'd first arrived this evening? Or as he'd watched and listened to her over dinner? Or perhaps when he had made love with her just now? Or maybe even before any of that? Possibly when he had first seen Nina in the gallery yesterday, and then spoken to her in the privacy of his office later that morning?

Whatever the reason—or when it had happened—his dinner invitation certainly had nothing to do with the irritation he felt at Dmitri Palitov's warning. If anything, being warned off by a woman's father—not that Rafe could ever remember meeting the father of any of the women he had been involved with in the past!—would normally have been enough to cause Rafe to retreat as far as possible in the opposite direction. Not because he would have been in the least concerned by that threat, but because he really didn't do complicated where women were concerned, and having a woman's father warn him off was definitely a complication.

Rafe had a feeling that this unexpected attraction to Nina Palitov was going to complicate the hell out of his life.

Nina drew in a shaking breath, knowing that her answer to Rafe's invitation should be no—and not because of the reason Rafe had just given. Oh, no doubt her father wouldn't exactly be pleased if she were to accept Rafe D'Angelo's dinner invitation, but it was a displeasure her father would have to deal with for once. After the two of them had their talk tomorrow he would know that she wasn't too thrilled to learn that he had warned Rafe off in the first place.

No, the reason Nina knew she should refuse Rafe's invitation had nothing to do with her father, and everything to do with her not being sure it was a good idea to allow herself to become any more attracted to Rafe than she already was. If she spent a whole evening alone with him she had no idea if she would be able to resist him at the end of the evening.

She wasn't a complete innocent, having believed herself in love a couple of times while she was at Stanford, both times with fellow students, one during her second year at university, the other one during her final year.

It hadn't taken her long, however, to realise she wasn't

really in love with either man, possibly because she had found them both less than exciting physically. So much so that she had wondered what all the fuss was about. Nor had she had any particular interest in repeating the experience once she had returned to New York.

Her response to Rafe just minutes ago, to his kisses and caresses, had been nothing like either of those earlier experiences. She had been breathless with arousal, hadn't wanted him to stop touching and kissing her, would have been perfectly happy if Rafe had just carried her off to her bedroom before stripping her completely naked and making love with her. She had ached for him to make love with her.

Just looking at him now, with that overlong dark hair tousled about that perfect, chiselled face, his black evening suit perfectly tailored to the broadness of his shoulders and muscled chest, his waist slender, and hips narrow above long legs, was enough to send a shiver of that same aching longing coursing through her own body.

He quirked one dark, mocking brow. 'Are you usually this indecisive?'

Nina's cheeks warmed with colour as she heard the rebuke beneath that mockery—implying, no doubt, that indecision was responsible for her father having taken over her life so completely.

'Perhaps I just don't think it a good idea to mix business with pleasure?'

Neither did Rafe, but he didn't seem to have any choice in the matter this time, not when it came to Nina Palitov. She was who she was, and he was determined to spend an evening alone with her. Bodyguards or no bodyguards! 'Yes or no, Nina?' he challenged between gritted teeth.

'Oh, okay—yes, I'll have dinner with you tomorrow evening!' She glared up at him impatiently.

Rafe held back his smile of triumph, merely nodding his satisfaction instead. 'I'll make the arrangements and call for you here tomorrow, at seven-thirty?'

She winced, and a frown appeared between those moss-green eyes. 'I'll need to know beforehand exactly where we're going.'

'Small rebellion over— Hey, it's okay, Nina,' he assured her gently as she instantly began to chew worriedly on her bottom lip. Lips that were still temptingly plumped from the kisses they had just shared. 'It really isn't a problem.'

'No?' Her eyes looked huge in the pallor of her face.

'No.' Rafe had already decided not to make life any more difficult for her than her father's stranglehold of security already made it for her. It was enough for Rafe, for now, that she had agreed to go out to dinner with him tomorrow evening. 'I'll let you know at the gallery tomorrow where we're going—I take it that Andy and Rich, or someone very like them, is going to check the place out before we arrive?'

'You make it sound so cloak and dagger.' She frowned.

Rafe shrugged. 'It lacks a certain spontaneity,' he acknowledged ruefully. 'But don't worry about it. We'll make it workable.'

'Thank you,' she breathed.

He looked at her curiously. 'For what?'

'For not—well, for not being difficult. A lot of men would be.'

'I'd hope I'm not like a lot of men, Nina—or even a random one,' Rafe added teasingly, in an effort to lighten the subject for her.

'Stop worrying.' He reached up to smooth the frown from between her brows before bending his head and lightly brushing his lips across hers before straightening. 'I'll see you at the gallery tomorrow?'

'Yes.'

'Smile, Nina, it might never happen,' he cajoled, as she still looked less than happy.

It was already happening as far as Nina was concerned; she was far too attracted to Rafe D'Angelo. Attracted enough that she had allowed him to make love to her.

Attracted enough that she was rebelling against some of the constraints imposed on her life by her father—something that had never happened before.

Attracted enough that she would have to keep reminding herself that no woman had ever succeeded in capturing and holding the long-term interest of the elusive Raphael D'Angelo. That there had only ever been a series of tall, leggy, blonde and sophisticated women, who apparently drifted in and out of his life—and his bed!—with sickening regularity.

And Nina knew herself to be only two of those things—tall and leggy!

Which didn't mean she couldn't enjoy this for exactly what it was: a flirtation on Rafe's part that might or might not eventually lead to them going to bed together.

She smiled as she straightened determinedly. 'I'm really fine, Rafe. And yes, I'll be at the gallery tomorrow.'

'Good.' He nodded his satisfaction with her answer. 'And now I think it's time I was going. There may be no bodyguards following you around tonight but I'm pretty sure the extensive security cameras in this building have already shown your father that I came into your apartment with you earlier but haven't left yet!' he added lightly as the two of them walked the short distance down the hallway to the door to her apartment.

Nina was pretty sure they had too.

Which wasn't to say she liked it, only that this level of security had been in her life for so long she had mainly ceased to even notice it. Maybe it was time she did.

And maybe meeting Rafe, and this attraction she felt towards him, were exactly the wake-up call she had needed to do something about changing it.

Rafe considered telephoning Michael once he got back to his own apartment twenty minutes later, and then dismissed the idea. His brother would be arriving in New York on Friday evening anyway, in time for the invitation-only gala opening of the Palitov jewellery collection on Saturday evening. The brothers attended any new exhibition presented in one of their three galleries. Gabriel wouldn't make it this time, but Michael would certainly be there.

And, amongst other things, Rafe was going to take the opportunity of Michael's presence to discuss a new business venture he had in mind for the Archangel galleries. Not too many people were aware of it, but Rafe was the new ideas man for the Archangel galleries, and always had been. And the reason people weren't aware of it was because Rafe was really quite modest. He didn't mind that the media had him tagged as the playboy.

Only maybe it was now time for that to change.

Rafe brought his thoughts up with a start, having no idea why he'd had them in the first place. Or why now.

It couldn't possibly be because of his attraction to Nina. Could it?

Damn it, he needed to concentrate on learning more about the enigmatic Dmitri Palitov, not his daughter.

Nina had said her father was in a wheelchair because he had been involved in an accident, which probably explained why he had become so reclusive. No doubt it was just as easy for Dmitri Palitov to run his business empire from his apartment on the fiftieth floor of a building he owned as it was to have an actual office in another part of the city.

But an accident didn't explain why Dmitri Palitov was so obsessive about security.

His daughter's security in particular.

CHAPTER FIVE

'I HAVEN'T EATEN here before,' Nina told Rafe as she glanced appreciatively at their surroundings. They had been seated at a secluded table near the window of a fashionable—and wildly exclusive—New York restaurant.

Situated on the top floor of one of New York's most prestigious skyscrapers, with three-hundred-and-sixty-degree views over the city, it was one of the in places for the rich and famous to enjoy themselves in relative privacy. Nina had spotted several easily recognisable TV personalities, as well as actresses and actors, as they were shown to their table. She even recognised a couple of politicians.

As she had said she would, Nina had spent the day at the gallery—most of the time vacillating between going out to dinner with Rafe this evening, as planned, or telling him she couldn't make it after all.

The latter hadn't been because she had received a particularly negative response from her father in regard to the date she had planned with Rafe for this evening; her father's mouth might have tightened with disapproval, but he seemed to know, from the stubbornness of Nina expression, not to comment further.

No, Nina's earlier trepidation, in regard to having dinner with Rafe, had been for a completely different reason. And that reason was Rafe D'Angelo himself.

Rafe was unlike any other man she had ever met. Confident and forceful, but not obnoxiously so, with a wicked sense of humour that was also teasing. He was intelligent without being pompous, and his bad-boy good looks were undiminished by the trappings of civilisation. The elegant black evening suit and snowy silk shirt and bow tie he was wearing this evening did little to temper that impression.

He also showed absolutely none of the awe for her father that so many other men did. Nina had been out to dinner with only three other men since her return to New York three years ago. Without exception all of those men had almost fallen over themselves in an effort to impress her father, with Nina's own preferences or dislikes coming a very poor second.

Rafe, on the other hand, was respectful to her father but at the same time not in the least overwhelmed by the Palitov power or wealth. No, Rafe was most definitely his own man: charming, worldly, wealthy, and confident of himself and his own abilities.

A dangerous combination to a woman who had always known the full force of the effect on other people of the wealth and power of the Palitov name.

'I heard this place was booked up weeks in advance,' she added conversationally, once the waiter had poured them each a glass of the pink champagne that had been delivered to their table the moment they sat down, the bottle now resting in a nest of ice in the bucket beside the table.

Rafe shrugged. 'The owner is a friend of mine.'

Nina gave a teasing smile. 'Was he a friend before you started eating here so often, or did that come later?' It wasn't the same restaurant Rafe had been photographed in with Jennifer Nichols, but Nina was pretty sure she had seen several other photographs on the Internet of him leaving this particular restaurant with other beautiful women.

Rafe shrugged. 'I knew Gerry before he opened this restaurant. Talking of which—he enjoyed having your two men come by earlier,' he added ruefully.

Nina eyed him uncertainly. 'I'm not sure if that's sarcasm or not?'

'Not,' Rafe drawled ruefully. 'Apparently they did a thorough sweep of the place, and then, because they weren't officially on duty for another couple of hours, and the restaurant was still closed, the three of them sat down together and played poker for an hour or so till opening time. Gerry loves playing poker. Especially when he wins,' he added dryly.

Nina chuckled. 'That sounds like Lawrence and Paul; they taught me to play poker when I was ten, and I started beating them when I was twelve.'

Rafe knew his eyes had widened, but otherwise he managed to keep his expression passive. 'You play poker with your bodyguards?'

'Not so much since I started winning.' She laughed.

'Remind me never to play strip poker with you,' he drawled dryly. 'Shouldn't you have still been playing with—oh, I don't know—dolls, or something equally girlish at that age?'

'Sexist!' Nina came back dryly. 'I never played with dolls, and certainly not aged twelve,' she added with a grimace. 'I was more interested in boys then than anything so childishly girlish.'

'And playing poker.' Yet more insight into the strangeness of Nina's upbringing, Rafe acknowledged with a frown. Not only had she grown up alone with her father, but her only other companions during those years appeared to have been her bodyguards.

'Only until I started winning,' she reminded him.

'Hmm.' He frowned. 'Gerry wanted me to thank you for letting your two men stand guard outside the main restaurant rather than inside it.'

'No doubt that's so that they can vet the people coming in.' Nina winced. 'I realise they can be a little intrusive.'

'I told you not to worry about it,' Rafe dismissed easily.

And she was trying, she really was. 'What are we celebrating?' She eyed the champagne curiously.

'Life?'

Nina smiled as she lifted her glass and chinked it against his before taking an appreciative sip; she loved pink champagne, and Rafe had ordered a bottle from her absolutely favourite vineyard. Coincidentally? Or had he known beforehand?

Rafe smiled as Nina gave him a suspicious glance. 'Guilty, as charged,' he drawled in answer to her unspoken question. 'I telephoned your father earlier today and asked him for the name of your favourite wine.'

Nina's eyes widened. 'You did?'

'Hmm.' Rafe rested his elbows on the table, his glass clasped loosely between his fingers as he looked at Nina through narrowed lids.

She looked absolutely stunning tonight. She wore a black sequined knee-length sheath of a dress that clung lovingly to the slenderness of her curves, but left her neck and arms bare. Only a pale green shadow on her lids, her lashes long and dark, a peachy blush to her cheeks, her lips coloured with a deeper peach lip gloss. Her hair was secured in a loose knot at her crown, leaving the long creamy column of her throat vulnerably bare.

Ironically, considering her father's unique and priceless jewellery collection, Nina wore no jewellery this evening. There was nothing to detract from the smooth perfection of her creamy pale peach skin, just a small pair of diamond ear studs.

Rafe had been fully aware that it had been that understated elegance and beauty, in contrast to the other over-jewelled and dramatically made-up women in the restaurant, that had caught the eye of every man in the room when the two of them entered the restaurant together. In response he had placed his arm about Nina's waist, drawing her tightly against his side as they crossed the room to their table.

Not possessively, exactly. Rafe had never felt possessive over a woman in his life. But he hadn't wanted any of those men to be under any illusion as to who Nina was with this evening. Or to have any doubts that she would be leaving with that same man at the end of the evening too.

Was that being possessive? Hell if Rafe knew. What he did know was that he hadn't in the least enjoyed having other men eyeing Nina so appreciatively.

She moistened those full and peach-coloured lips with a nervous sweep of her tongue. 'You spoke to my father today…?' she repeated slowly.

Rafe raised dark brows. 'A courtesy call, to thank him for dinner yesterday evening.'

'That's all?'

He shrugged. 'I told you, I also wanted to know the name and year of your favourite wine.'

Which, Nina accepted, all sounded innocent enough. Except last night her father had warned Rafe to stay away from her, a warning Rafe had taken exception to. And now she was expected to believe that earlier today Rafe had made a thank-you call to her father, and that her father had happily supplied the younger man with the name of her favourite wine for when he took her out to dinner this evening?

She eyed him sceptically. 'And my father just gave it to you?'

'Your happiness is very important to him.' Rafe took another sip of his champagne, those predatory golden eyes quietly watchful over the rim of the glass.

'Rafe—'

'Relax, Nina,' he cut in soothingly. 'Let's look at the menus and order our dinner,' he added as the waiter brought the menus to their table. 'And then, if you still want to, you can ask me more about my conversation with your father earlier today.'

Oh, Nina would still want to. Just as she couldn't help wondering if Rafe's telephone conversation with her father today wasn't the reason her father had made no objections when Nina had told him of her date with Rafe D'Angelo this evening. It certainly explained her father's lack of surprise.

'Spit it out, Nina,' Rafe drawled once they had made their food selections and the waiter had unobtrusively topped up their champagne glasses before leaving them alone together. 'I can tell by your worried expression that you're still questioning my motives for telephoning your father earlier today,' he supplied as she glanced across at him enquiringly.

Nina looked at him beneath lowered lashes. 'Am I such an open book?'

'Hardly!' Rafe chuckled softly. This woman had been

a mystery to him from the first, and the more he came to know her, it seemed the more of a mystery she became.

His forays on the Internet had told him that Nina and her father had lived alone together since she was five years old, and that she had spent her earlier years being educated at home. Her childhood seemed to have been spent exclusively with her wheelchair-bound father, and the muscled men that made up her security detail—making it doubly amazing that she had managed to escape and attend university at all.

Rafe was even more convinced, since meeting Dmitri Palitov, that the other man must have been having heart palpitations over that one. At the same time Rafe couldn't help but admire Nina for having had the strength to break out of that protective cocoon.

And yet, having broken free for three years, Nina had then stepped back into that repressive ring of security when she'd returned to New York. Admittedly she now had her own apartment in the building her father owned, but it was still very much under her father's protection. And the design work she did was always within her father's corporation.

Rafe's efforts last night to find out more about Dmitri Palitov had hit wall after wall after Nina was five and her mother had died. Nor could Rafe find any record of Anna Palitov's death, or the reason for it. As there had been only the briefest mention made of the accident just weeks later that had resulted in Dmitri Palitov being in a wheelchair. A car accident that had apparently killed two of the three men travelling in the other car.

Mystery, after mystery, after mystery.

And Nina, slightly shy, vibrantly beautiful, sexy as hell, as well as intelligent, and incredibly talented in her designs, was front and centre of that mystery.

'I didn't telephone your father, or tell him of our dinner date, with any idea of challenging his warning last
night, Nina,' Rafe assured her softly now.

'No?' She winced.

'No,' he replied evenly, having known it would, but
hoped it wouldn't, be her conclusion regarding his actions. 'I would hope I'm neither that petty nor that vin-
dictive.'

A delicate blush coloured her cheeks at the reproof
in Rafe's tone.

'Then why did you tell him?'

'So that you didn't have to.' Rafe reached over and
placed one of his hands on the top of hers as it rested
on the tabletop. 'Nina, I'm fully aware of how close you
and your father are, and the last thing I want is to be the
cause of any tension between the two of you. What I do
want is for the two of us to get to know each other better,
and I have no intention of doing that by leaving you to
be the one who has to do the explaining to your father.'

Nina felt the sting of tears in her eyes. Rafe was already too much for one woman to handle: too wickedly
handsome, too charming, too amusing, definitely too
sexually attractive for his own good. Or, as she had realised last night, her own good.

And she had been totally physically aware of Rafe this
evening from the moment she had opened her apartment
door and looked at him standing out in the hallway. His
hair had still been damp from the shower he must have
taken, he had obviously shaved too, but his beard was
so dark there was still a sexy shadow along his jawline.
And as for the warmth in those golden eyes as his gaze
roved slowly over her...

Adding understanding and compassion to Rafe's already long list of attractions was just being unfair to any woman.

And yet Nina had no doubts that whatever Rafe had said to her father during their telephone call earlier today, it had helped pave the way for her own conversation with her father this evening.

'Dmitri and I may not be altogether sure that we like each other yet,' Rafe continued dryly, 'but I think we respect each other. Which is a start.'

Yes, Nina could appreciate that her father was old-fashioned enough to have appreciated the fact that Rafe had been the one to tell him of their dinner date this evening, even if he hadn't particularly liked or approved of it. Her father admired strength, respected that strength, and Rafe had it in abundance.

She gave a rueful grimace. 'I'm sorry I was so suspicious of your motives just now.'

'Let's not spend the whole evening apologising to each other, Nina,' Rafe cut across that apology, giving her hand one last squeeze before sitting back as the waiter placed the first course in front of them.

'So tell me what you do at Archangel,' Nina prompted once the waiter had departed.

'What do I do?'

'Yes.' She nodded. 'I know that you and your two brothers manage the galleries, but I'm sure that doesn't take up all of your time,' she prompted interestedly.

Which was how Rafe came to find himself telling Nina more about the work he did, and about coming up with new ideas for Archangel. He told her some anecdotes from his childhood, growing up in a family of three boys.

'Your poor mother!' Nina laughed softly after Rafe had related one of those stories of his childhood, involving himself and Gabriel placing a frog in their grandmother's bed when she came to stay during the summer when he was eleven. 'Michael wasn't involved too?' she prompted curiously as she took a sip of the coffee that had been served to signal the end of their meal.

Rafe gave a shake of his head. 'Even at twelve Michael was the serious one, the responsible one.'

Nina remembered that aloof seriousness from that one occasion she had met Michael D'Angelo. 'Maybe he didn't feel he had a choice, with two mischievous younger brothers?'

Rafe frowned as he seemed to give the suggestion some thought, now wondering if perhaps his older brother chose to live behind a public mask too.

'I've never thought of it quite like that before, but you could be right,' Rafe conceded slowly. 'And talking of Michael, I spoke to him this afternoon, too.'

Her brows rose. 'He's back in New York?'

Rafe shook his head. 'Still in Paris. We spoke on a conference call.'

Nina's brows rose. 'You have been busy today!'

He frowned. 'Didn't the things I've just told you show that I'm busy every day?'

Yes, they had, Nina acknowledged with an inner glow, not sure why Rafe had chosen to answer her questions so candidly, but pleased that he had, now knowing there was so much more to this man, a depth that others wouldn't know was there.

She eyed him teasingly. 'I believe it's the newspapers who prefer to report on your night-time activities rather than the daytime ones!'

'They take delight in reporting what they think are my night-time activities,' Rafe corrected dryly.

'All those photographs of you out with beautiful

women are just a figment of the press's imagination?'
she prompted.

Unfortunately, Rafe knew they weren't. And worst of
all, of course, was the one of him with Jennifer Nichols
two nights ago, when he had refused to cancel his prior
arrangements to have dinner with Nina and her father.

'My main reason for talking to Michael...' Rafe
abruptly changed the subject '...was because I wanted to
see what he thought about my suggestion of asking you to
design new display cabinets for all three of the galleries.'

'Me?' She was obviously stunned by the suggestion.

'Why not?' He frowned at Nina's reaction. 'The display cabinets you designed for your father are elegantly
beautiful in their simplicity. The same elegance and simplicity that we aim for at Archangel.'

'Well. Yes. I've noticed that these past few days.
But...' She was obviously flustered. 'I already have a
job.'

'Working for your father.'

Nina could hear the disapproval in Rafe's tone. Perhaps deserved, after all those years she had spent attaining her design degree from Stanford.

But Rafe didn't understand. No one did. Because most
people, Rafe included, had no idea what had happened to
them nineteen years ago. Nina was well aware that her
father had used the Palitov wealth and power to make certain not all the events of that time were ever made public.

'Don't you have any hopes and dreams of your own,
Nina?' Rafe pressed determinedly, refusing to back down
on the subject. 'An ambition to do something more with
your life than stand in your father's shadow?'

She gasped, her face visibly paling at this attack coming so quickly after Rafe had talked to her so candidly.
Or perhaps that was the reason for the attack? She very

much doubted that Rafe spoke that candidly about himself to many people. 'That was uncalled for,' she murmured softly.

'But true?'

'Thank you for a lovely dinner, Rafe, but I think perhaps it's time I left.' Nina turned away, the bareness of her shoulders defensively stiff as she slowly laid her napkin down on the table beside her empty coffee cup, sure now that Rafe was being deliberately challenging. Because he had so completely let his guard down with her?

Rafe's mouth had thinned. 'I'm driving you home.'

'Lawrence and Paul will take me home.'

Rafe gave a slow, determined shake of his head. 'I drove you here. I'm driving you home.'

'Why?' Her eyes glittered deeply green. 'So that you can insult me some more? Because I asked too many questions? Or because you answered them?' she added astutely as she stood up, black clutch bag in her hand.

Rafe stood up too, grasping her arm as she would have brushed past him on her way to the door. 'And is this what you do, Nina?' he challenged softly. 'Run away every time someone says something that strikes a little too close to home?'

Tears glistened in her eyes as she looked up at him. 'Run home to Daddy, do you mean?'

He winced at the sight of those tears swimming in her pained green eyes. 'I didn't say that.'

'You meant it, though,' Nina said knowingly, attempting to shake off his hold on her arm but not succeeding. 'You're causing a scene, Rafe,' she muttered as she noticed several people at the neighbouring tables were giving discreetly curious glances in their direction.

Not surprising really. The two of them had obviously been getting on so well, talking and laughing together, all the time with that underlying edge of flirtation and awareness, as they ate their delicious meal, and then lingered over coffee, and now this.

And of course Nina had ambitions and hopes and dreams of her own. Lots of them. And one of them had been to go to Stanford. Which she had done.

But she hadn't taken into account how frail her father would be when she returned to New York to live three years later, a frailty she felt partly responsible for, because she knew how much of a strain it had been for him, a worry, while she was away. At the time, the most she had felt comfortable insisting upon was that she be allowed to have her own apartment rather than continue to live with her father in the penthouse apartment.

But that didn't mean that she didn't still long to start her own design business, to be able to take commissions like the one Rafe had just offered her at the Archangel galleries, in London and Paris as well as here. Just thinking of accepting such a commission made her heart soar with excitement.

But it was never going to happen. Not while her father was alive, anyway, and Nina wanted him with her for many more years to come.

'Careful, Rafe—' Nina fell back on mockery as her defence '—or the next thing you'll see in the newspapers is a photograph of you manhandling a woman in your friend's restaurant!'

'Gerry doesn't allow the press inside his restaurant,' he rasped tautly.

So much for mockery! 'Nevertheless, I would appreciate it if you would let go of my arm.' She met his gaze challengingly.

And Rafe would have appreciated it if he could have

just managed to get through a single evening with Nina without the two of them arguing.

Maybe he shouldn't have brought up the subject of having Nina design some display cabinets for the gallery yet. Perhaps he shouldn't challenge her about having hopes and dreams of her own, rather than those imposed on her by her father's security. He certainly shouldn't have accused Nina of running away when the subject became too personal for her!

So why had he?

Because, as she had intimated, she had got too close, Rafe realised. By answering her questions, he had allowed her to see the astute businessman, the 'new ideas' man, behind the façade of the playboy. And it had unsettled him. He'd never allowed any woman to question him so deeply about his work or his family.

But having Nina walk out on him in this way unsettled him more!

'We'll talk about this in the car,' he told her stiffly.

'I told you that I will ride back with Lawrence and Paul.'

'Oh, no, Nina, you don't get to tell me anything when it comes to who's taking you home tonight,' he assured softly, maintaining a hold on her arm as he strode across the restaurant.

He gave Gerry a stiff nod as they paused in the reception area to collect Nina's cashmere wrap, knowing, by his friend's understanding nod as Rafe draped that wrap about the stiffness of Nina's shoulders, that Gerry was more than happy for Rafe to settle the bill at his convenience. Which certainly wasn't now. Anything but Rafe's complete attention and Nina was likely to just walk out of here and not look back.

'We're going to my apartment,' he briskly informed

the two security men waiting near the lifts as he maintained a firm grip on Nina's arm. 'No doubt you're aware of exactly where that is?' he added tersely as he and Nina stepped into one of the lifts together, Rafe pressing the button to close the doors and leaving the two men to follow behind in the second lift.

'Rafe.'

'Not now, Nina,' he bit out through clenched teeth.

'But…'

'Please, Nina.' Rafe's gaze was rapier sharp as he looked down at her. 'I'm trying my damnedest not to—'

He drew in a deep, controlling breath. 'All I want right now is to get you out of here so that we can go to the privacy of my apartment.'

His car was being brought to the front of the building even as they stepped outside. No doubt Gerry had called down to the valets in the underground garage as soon as Rafe and Nina stepped into the lift together. The valet got quickly out of the car to open the passenger door for Nina to get inside, at the same time as the two bodyguards rushed out of the building behind them and hurried off to get their own car from where it was parked further down the block.

The silent drive to Rafe's apartment—doggedly followed by the black limousine occupied by Lawrence and Paul—gave Rafe ample time to think of that last conversation in the restaurant. To accept that he was definitely responsible for the current tension that existed between himself and Nina. And after he had previously decided he would be the one person in Nina's life who didn't cause her hassle or tension.

'I'm sorry,' he murmured on a sigh.

'I thought we weren't going to spend the evening apologising to each other?'

'This one needs to be said. My remark was out of line.'

'It's okay,' Nina said softly.

Rafe gave her a brief glance, his jaw tightening as he saw the tracks of the tears that were still falling down the paleness of her cheeks, before he turned his gaze sharply back to manoeuvring through the late night traffic clogging up the city's streets. 'No, it isn't,' he bit out, disgusted with himself.

No, it wasn't, Nina acknowledged miserably, having now realised that this evening, with Rafe, an evening that had started out with such promise, and which she had been enjoying immensely, was now going to end as disastrously as those dinners she'd had with three other men since returning home to New York.

She had hoped tonight would be different, because Rafe was different from anyone else she had ever known, their conversation this evening showing her he wasn't just the playboy he wanted everyone else to think that he was.

But she could see now that it wasn't going to work. That although he had no intention of sucking up to her father and ignoring what Nina wanted, as those other men had, her attraction to Rafe was pulling her in another direction completely, and one that she knew would ultimately cause her father further heartache. And that was something Nina absolutely refused to do; her father had suffered enough.

And going to Rafe's apartment with him wasn't going to change any of that. No matter how volatile she knew her physical reaction to him was...

CHAPTER SIX

'FEELING BETTER?'

'Yes, thank you,' Nina confirmed huskily as she looked up at Rafe after taking a sip of the brandy he had insisted on pouring for both of them once they reached his apartment.

In the end, Nina hadn't been able to resist accompanying him there; if this was to be their one and only date, as it probably would be, then she intended making the most of it.

The modern décor of Rafe's apartment had come as something of a surprise to her, even a disappointment, with its colour scheme of black, silver and white. The walls in the sitting room were white, as was the carpet, with a black leather sofa and chairs, and a glass coffee table, only the original artwork on the walls and the fantastic view of New York outside the huge windows to prevent it from appearing utilitarian.

It certainly reflected none of the sensuality or larger than life personality of the man who occupied it.

'It's a family-owned apartment,' Rafe dismissed as he saw her curiosity. 'Whichever of the brothers is in New York at the time uses it.'

She blinked. 'Do you change locations a lot, then?'

'Every two months or so, sometimes more often.' Rafe

shrugged. 'Depends what's happening at the time. We have an exhibition coming up in Paris next month, and, with Gabriel away on his honeymoon, Michael decided to take over in Paris for a while. He'll be flying over here on Friday for the gala opening on Saturday, of course.'

Nina knew they were both just talking for the sake of it, that Rafe was trying to put her at her ease. 'My father will appreciate that.' She nodded.

'Michael wouldn't think of not being there.'

And yet Michael had no reservations in leaving Rafe in charge of her father's exhibition. Further proof that Nina really shouldn't believe all that she read about Rafe in the newspapers, that, as she had realised this evening, he really wasn't just the playboy the press had made him out to be.

Rafe placed his glass down on the coffee table before coming down on his haunches beside the chair where Nina sat. He took her free hand in his. 'I really am sorry about earlier. For making you cry,' he told her gruffly. 'I shouldn't have pushed you so hard.'

'It isn't your fault.' Her hand shook slightly inside his as she gave a shake of her head. 'You can't possibly understand, and I can't explain, either,' she added emotionally.

Those golden eyes narrowed. 'Why can't you?'

'It isn't possible.'

His jaw tightened. 'I repeat, why not?'

'Because it isn't my story to tell.'

Rafe had already guessed as much, just as he now believed this story had something to do with whatever had happened to the Palitov family nineteen years ago. When Nina's mother had died, and Dmitri Palitov had been involved in the car accident that had resulted in his being in a wheelchair for the rest of his life.

The timing of those two events, just weeks apart, and Nina's refusal to talk about them, made Rafe wonder if they might actually be linked by more than just Dmitri's distraction at the loss of his wife.

And it mattered to him, Rafe realised. Knowing, what kept the beautiful and talented Nina hidden away from the world mattered to him.

As did the woman herself?

The only thing that mattered at the moment was learning why, whatever might have happened nineteen years ago, Nina continued to allow her life to be so restricted.

Why Dmitri Palitov kept his daughter so protected and sheltered he was in danger of suffocating her.

Rafe had even wondered, as he had allowed his imagination free rein the night before, and having found no actual proof of Anna Palitov's death, if she hadn't just chosen to leave her husband and daughter nineteen years ago. It would certainly go a long way to explaining why Dmitri had become so determined not to lose Nina too.

Nina's smile was sad as she saw the frustrated anger in Rafe's expression; the flash of temper in those amazing golden eyes, chiselled lips thinned as he obviously raged an inner battle with his impatience at her refusal to talk to him, to tell him, the reason she refused to break away from her father's protection.

Nina had no actual memories of what had happened nineteen years ago. She had been five years old at the time, and only knew what had really happened because her father had explained it to her when she was ten, old enough to understand that horrendous sequence of events that had shaped their lives.

And Nina could still remember her father's pain that day, as if it had been just minutes ago rather than five years.

Oh, Nina had been fully aware that her mother had disappeared from her life when she was five. She had cried over it, had pleaded and thrown temper tantrums as she demanded to know where her mother had gone. A demand her father had assuaged by assuring her that her mother hadn't wanted to leave them, that she'd had no choice.

But it had been another five years before her father had explained exactly why Anna had left them.

Kidnapped.

Ransomed.

A ransom Dmitri had gladly paid in his desire to have his beloved wife returned to him, as he had also complied with the kidnappers' demand that he not inform the police or the press of the kidnapping, or his wife would die.

The payment of that ransom hadn't stopped the kidnappers from killing their hostage, anyway. From killing Nina's kind and beautiful mother, and Dmitri's beloved wife.

Or stopped Nina's father from hunting down the three men responsible.

And when he finally found those three men her father had contacted them and arranged to meet with them, only for their two cars to be involved in an accident that had resulted in two of those three men being killed outright, and putting Dmitri in a wheelchair for the rest of his life.

And Nina had always had her doubts as to how that accident had occurred, had always suspected—but never dared ask—that her father had intended those three men to die that day, as retribution for taking his beloved Anna's life.

Which was why Nina knew she could never explain, never tell anyone else about the events of nineteen years ago, without also implicating her father in the death of at least two of the men who had taken Anna from them both. She had always shied away from asking what had become of the third man.

She couldn't explain that to Rafe. She wouldn't. Even if it meant that she now had to allow Rafe, a man she liked and was so attracted to, to walk away from her without a single backward glance.

She drew in a deep, controlling breath before forcing a smile to her lips. 'I think it's time I was leaving.'

Rafe had had an idea that was where all Nina's concentrated thought was going to lead. 'You're running away again, Nina,' he reproved gently.

'Yes,' she confirmed without apology.

He frowned. 'You don't have to leave.'

'Yes,' she sighed. 'I really think that I do.'

Rafe gave a slow shake of his head. 'I don't want you to.' And he didn't.

In fact, Rafe could never remember wanting anything as much as he now wanted Nina to stay, here with him, in this apartment, in his bed.

He reached out and gently took the brandy glass from Nina's unresisting fingers before placing that glass beside his own on the coffee table. Turning back to her and taking both of her hands into his, his gaze seeking and capturing hers as he looked down at her intently. 'Don't go, Nina,' he encouraged gruffly. 'Stay here with me tonight.'

Nina's breath caught in her throat, her heart beating loudly, erratically, in her chest, both at the words Rafe had just spoken, and the intensity of the desire she could see burning in the depths of those glittering golden eyes that looked so intently into hers. 'You'll be disappointed.'

'What?' Rafe stared at her incredulously, obviously startled by her reply.

Heat coloured Nina's cheeks as she avoided meeting

that shocked gaze. 'I—' She moistened suddenly dry lips with a sweep of her tongue. 'I'm not experienced, Rafe. I'm not a virgin either,' she hastened to add, so there should be no misunderstandings. 'But I'm not experienced, not like the other women you've—' She ceased speaking as he pressed his fingertips gently against her lips.

'Nina, all that matters here and now is the two of us,' he assured gruffly. 'No one else, and certainly not the past, but what we both want now. And I want you very much,' he added huskily. 'Do you want me?'

Too much!

Nina had wanted Rafe from the moment she had looked at him that first day, as he stood in the doorway of the gallery in the east wing of Archangel.

It had been so obvious that day that Rafe had assumed she was just another one of her father's workmen, and she had very much enjoyed taking off her baseball cap to release her fiery red hair down her back, in order to shatter that illusion.

Because looking at Rafe had awoken dormant feelings inside her, a physical awareness, a desire that had caused her body to hum with the need for him to see her as a desirable woman.

Exactly the way Rafe was looking at her now. His golden eyes warm with the same desire that coursed through her own veins, an aroused flush to the sharp blade of his cheekbones, those chiselled lips parted, as if he was just waiting for her to say yes so that he could kiss her.

And God knew Nina wanted him to kiss her. Wanted Rafe in a way she had never wanted any other man. To kiss him. To touch him. To make love with him.

And why shouldn't she do just that? Why shouldn't she

take this one night with him? Lose herself in that desire, that arousal, and enjoy Rafe in the way she would never be able to do again?

Because Nina already knew that had to be the ultimate outcome of this evening. That Rafe was far too intelligent, too intensely curious about the past, her past, for her to ever risk incriminating her father by answering any of Rafe's questions.

She moistened her lips with the tip of her tongue before answering, her gaze remaining unwavering on his.

'Yes, I want you, Rafe,' she answered softly, steadily, allowing no room for doubts in her mind. She would take this one night of pleasure, enjoy it, revel in it, with no expectations of anything other than tonight. Men did it all the time, Rafe did it all the time, so why shouldn't she?

'Right now,' she added determinedly.

'Good girl.' It wasn't triumph, but satisfaction, that flared in those golden eyes as he straightened beside her before holding out one of his hands to her invitingly.

Nina placed her own hand unhesitatingly into his as she rose to her feet in front of him. Rafe kept possession of that hand as they turned and walked out of the room together and down the hallway to his bedroom.

Nina felt no reservations, no doubts, as Rafe maintained that hold on her hand as he switched on one of the bedside lamps before turning to cup either side of her face, gazing down searchingly into her eyes before his head lowered towards hers.

'You are so beautiful,' he murmured huskily.

'Kiss me, Rafe,' she encouraged.

'Your mouth has been driving me insane since the first moment I looked at you,' he acknowledged gruffly.

She blinked. 'My mouth?'

'You have the most delicious, lusciously pouting lips,

and I've been imagining kissing them, and having them kiss me, since the moment I first met you. Everywhere,' he groaned.

Her cheeks warmed with colour. 'How can that possibly be true, when you went out with, made love to, another woman that same evening?'

'I didn't,' he drawled. 'Oh, I went out to dinner with her, but bedding her was a different matter, when the woman I wanted was a tall and fiery redhead who enjoys challenging me.'

Nina felt warmed inside just knowing that Rafe hadn't been intimate with Jennifer Nichols two nights ago. Because it was her that he wanted. Her. Nina Palitov. 'In that case, I think I would very much enjoy being kissed and kissing you. Everywhere…'

So would Rafe.

To hell with his rules and the complications of being involved with a woman like Nina; he wanted her. And those complications if that was the only way he could have her!

He continued to cradle the warmth of Nina's cheeks as he kissed her slowly, lingering for long heart-pounding minutes as he sipped and tasted those luscious lips that had taunted and tempted him these past three days. Nina returned the warmth, the heat of those kisses, as her hands glided up his shirt-covered chest beneath his jacket.

Rafe hadn't thought, hadn't dared to hope, that the evening would end like this. End? Damn it, this wasn't the end of him and Nina, but the beginning.

He continued to kiss her, those kisses becoming hungrier, wilder, more heated, as he reached up and took the clip from her hair, allowing those fiery red curls to cascade down the length of her spine. He shrugged out of his dinner jacket and let it fall to the floor. Nina groaned softly in her throat as her body now curved intimately into and against his, her hands now roaming restlessly over his muscled back.

Not close enough. They weren't nearly close enough for Rafe's liking. The barrier of their clothes had to go. He needed to see, to feel the heat of Nina's delicious curves, ached to taste those succulent breasts again, to hear Nina's soft cries of pleasure as he laved those breasts with his tongue and nibbled them with his teeth, before suckling deeply.

His lips raked down her throat in a heated caress as he slid the zip to her gown down the length of her spine, tasting her creamy flesh as he slipped the straps of her gown down her arms before letting it fall to the floor.

'Amazing.' Rafe breathed raggedly as Nina stood before him wearing only a pair of minuscule black lace panties and her high-heeled black shoes, her hair a wild fiery red tumble over her shoulders and breasts.

'You like?' Nina prompted shyly.

That heated gaze roamed over her hungrily. 'Oh, I definitely like!' Rafe assured gruffly. 'Take off the rest, Nina,' he encouraged gruffly.

'I was thinking of you when I wore these,' she revealed huskily as she stepped out of the high-heeled shoes before sliding the black panties down her thighs and dropping them on the carpet beside her gown. She was totally exposed to Rafe now, but not in the least self-conscious as she saw the desire for her burning in those glittering golden eyes. 'Because I wanted this to happen.'

His gaze flicked up to her face, studying her for long timeless moments before he nodded his satisfaction with whatever he saw in her expression. 'In that case, I think it only fair I should be naked too, don't you?' he mur-

mured as he stepped back, arms held slightly away from
his body in invitation.

Nina had never undressed a man before. Those two
previous encounters had been hurried and unsatisfying,
when neither she nor either of those two men had even
been completely undressed. Her fingers shook slightly as
she removed Rafe's bow tie before unfastening the but-
tons of his shirt, pushing the white silk down his arms as
she gazed her fill of the bareness of Rafe's wide shoulders and muscled chest. His skin there the same olive
tone as his face and hands, with a sprinkling of dark
hair that covered the flat bronze coins of his nipples, and
formed a vee as it tapered down the muscled flatness of
his abdomen before disappearing beneath the waistband
of his trousers.

'All of it, Nina,' he groaned achingly as he stepped
out of his shoes.

Her hands shook even more as she unfastened his trousers before sliding down the zip and allowing them to
fall to the floor, gasping as she saw the long bulge of his
shaft pressing impatiently against his black boxers. She
glanced up at Rafe, before quickly looking away again
as she saw the increased heat of the desire burning in
those golden eyes.

She could do this. She needed to do this. Needed to
be with Rafe, to touch and caress him.

She dropped smoothly to her knees in front of him,
Rafe's skin warm to the touch as she hooked her fingers
into the waistband of those black boxers, before easing
them down and off, baring his arousal.

Rafe was so utterly beautiful, his body as perfect as
a huge bronzed statue.

Nina placed one of her hands on Rafe's thigh, the other
about the thickness of his shaft as she lowered her head,

her tongue flicking out to lap, to taste the salty sweetness of the moisture coating the engorged tip. Encouraged by his low groans of pleasure as his hands moved out to grasp her shoulders, she parted her lips and took him completely into her mouth.

Rafe could barely breathe past the pleasure that engulfed him the moment he felt the lushness of Nina's lips parting before she took him inside the burning heat of her mouth, and then deeper still, taking him to the back of her throat, before moving back again until just the bulbous tip remained imprisoned in that burning heat, her tongue a torturous caress about the rim just below the exposed head, only to repeat that pleasurable lapping of her tongue as she sucked on him greedily, taking Rafe further, deeper down her throat, with each successive motion.

She repeated that caress again and again, humming softly beneath her breast as she lapped and sucked, the pleasure becoming overwhelming, until Rafe knew he couldn't take any more, that he was on the edge of exploding in her mouth.

'No more, Nina!' he groaned achingly as he gently eased her away from him, laughing gruffly as he saw the pout of disappointment on her lips as she looked up at him. 'It's going to be over too quickly for me if I allow you to continue doing that,' he explained huskily as he bent to sweep Nina up in his arms before carrying her over to the bed.

'It's my turn to explore and taste you now,' he assured as he laid her gently down onto the brown pillows and bedcover. Nina appearing a creamily skinned red-haired goddess against that darkness as Rafe moved onto the bed beside her.

Nina's back arched invitingly off the bed as Rafe's

head lowered and his lips parted to capture one hard, engorged nipple before suckling that hardness deep into the heat of his mouth, his hand moving to cup and caress its twin, causing a gush of heated moisture to dampen the swollen lips between her thighs as Rafe's other hand moved caressingly, unerringly, down to her parted thighs to stroke the swollen engorged nubbin hidden there, the dual assault on Nina's senses causing her to cry out as an orgasm immediately ripped through and over her in burning, rippling waves.

Rafe continued those caresses as Nina arched into her climax, suckling deeply on her nipple, deepening the stroke of his fingers as he felt the gushing of her juices against them, lightly squeezing her clitoris between his fingers as he continued to milk and prolong that orgasm until he was sure Nina had taken, enjoyed, every last gasping shudder of her pleasure.

She was so responsive, so open to him as Rafe slid down her body to rest his shoulders between her parted thighs, his hands moving up to capture, caress, pinch her nipples as he lowered his head to lap up the nectar of her juices. The lips there swollen and open, begging for the thrust of his tongue inside her, and causing that channel to ripple and contract as a second, more intensely pro-longed orgasm now caused her to arch her thighs into the deep thrusting rhythm of his tongue. Nina groaned his name over and over again as she came against his mouth.

'I want you inside me, Rafe,' Nina gasped as she reached down to entangle her fingers in his hair, mind-less with that need after experiencing, not just her first ever orgasm but also a second one, her channel still con-tracting greedily as it hungered for more.

'I need you inside me,' she demanded, groaning achingly at the sight of her own juices slicked across Rafe's lips as he raised his head to look up at her.

She whimpered softly in her throat as he rasped his tongue lingeringly over her sensitive nubbin once more before moving up her body, the silky hair on his chest rasping across the swollen nubbin between her splayed thighs, and then her sensitive nipples, as he laid his weight on her, his elbows either side of her head as he looked down at her searchingly.

'So, so beautiful,' he groaned, his hands cradled either side of her face as he kissed her again, deeply, hungrily, the erotic thrust of his tongue filling Nina's mouth with the taste of her own juices even as she felt the nudge of his shaft against her , parting her as his hardness slid inch by slow inch inside those sensitive tissues, the stretching, filling sensation an exquisite pleasure in itself, before he began to stroke slowly inside her, causing Nina to break the kiss as she gasped at each successive slow thrust, the pleasure building, rising, overwhelming in its intensity.

Rafe buried his face in her throat, lips grazing her flesh, his breathing ragged as he continued those slow and measured thrusts. He was threatening to drive Nina insane with the ache building higher and higher inside her.

'Harder, Rafe!' she gasped. 'Oh, please, harder!' she groaned as her nails dug into Rafe's shoulders, her legs curving over the backs of his thighs, pulling him into her as she met his hard thrusts, her body contracting about the long length of him as he filled her completely, her inner muscles squeezing, milking that length as he withdrew, causing Rafe to groan through clenched teeth with each new plunge, until he finally lost control and thrust faster, harder, into that slick heat.

Nina gave a guttural scream, her head thrashing from

side to side on the pillow as she felt another release tearing through her, more intense, more overwhelming even than the last two. She heard Rafe's harsh groan as her muscles tightened about him, clenching, squeezing the long length of his shaft as she convulsed in climax. His back arching, head thrown back, dark hair wild about his shoulders as the intensity of that golden gaze captured and held hers as his own release exploded into her in hot, thick jets, intensifying and prolonging Nina's own release as that heat hit the opening to her womb, filling her, completing her.

Rafe woke the following morning with the feel of the warmth of sun shining on his closed lids, and a smile on his lips. Nina was the reason for that smile as he remembered the night of passion they had just spent together. Hours and hours of making love, their hunger for each other seemingly insatiable.

He had gathered Nina's boneless body up in his arms after the first time, before drawing back the bedclothes and cuddling her beneath them as they fell asleep in each other's arms. But they had woken and made love twice more during the night, slowly, deliciously, wildly, each time becoming more attuned to each other's needs and desires, murmuring encouragements and gasps as they shared their pleasure in each other.

An intensity of pleasure Rafe knew he had never experienced before, with any woman.

A remembered intensity of pleasure that now made Rafe's smile widen as he thought of spending the morning in bed with Nina, or maybe the whole day. He was nowhere near to satisfying the intensity of the desire he felt for her.

Breakfast first, though. He needed to ensure Nina was

fed if they were going to make love all day. Besides, Nina would look sexy as hell walking about the apartment wearing one of his white silk shirts.

As it was, the lack of movement on her side of the king-sized bed told him that she was still sleeping deeply. No doubt she was exhausted after all that nocturnal activity!

Rafe's smile deepened at the thought of waking her, of slowly kissing those luscious lips while caressing that long, lithe body before thrusting deeply, languidly, into the welcoming heat of her sensitive and caressing body until they both gasped out their release.

He rolled over in the bed. 'Nina, I— What the...?'

The other side of the bed was empty, only the indentation in the pillow and the slight warmth of the sheets to show that Nina had been lying there beside him a short time ago.

'Nina?' Rafe called softly as he threw back the bed-clothes and got out of bed, padding barefoot and naked out into the hallway as he received no answer from the adjoining bedroom. 'I'm supposed to be the one to make you breakfast,' he teased as he entered the kitchen.

The empty kitchen.

And the rest of the apartment proved to be just as empty as Rafe moved from room to room in search of her.

'Damn it!' he finally muttered angrily as he re-entered the bedroom and realised that Nina's clothes and shoes were no longer on the floor where they had been discarded last night, that there wasn't a single item of her clothing in the bedroom to show that she had ever been there at all.

Because she'd left the bed, the apartment, and Rafe, before he had even woken up.

CHAPTER SEVEN

'WHAT THE HELL did you think you were doing?'

Nina's fingers stilled in arranging her father's jewellery collection in one of the open cabinets as she heard the sound of Rafe's rasping and angry voice behind her. She stood up slowly, her gaze wary as she turned to see that Rafe was indeed angry, if the furious glitter in his eyes and the nerve pulsing in his tensely clenched jaw were any indication.

There wasn't so much as a hint of the passionate and indulgent lover she had spent the night with.

A night of such an intensity of mind-blowing pleasure that it had been an absolute revelation to Nina. It made a complete nonsense of her two previous experiences; she definitely knew what all the fuss was about now!

Rafe had been a tender, fierce and erotic lover, bringing her to climax after climax as he explored and claimed every inch of her body, in the same way that he had allowed, encouraged her, to explore and pleasure every inch of his.

Nina blushed now just remembering the intimacies the two of them had shared during the night. No part of her, not a single inch, left untouched, unsatisfied, by Rafe's caressing hands and mouth, and she was sure she now knew his body more intimately than she knew her own.

'It's okay,' she huskily assured Rich and Andy as she saw they had stepped forward protectively, heads turned towards Rafe as he stood in the doorway of the gallery looking every inch the wealthy and sophisticated Rafe D'Angelo. He was dressed in his custom tailored charcoal suit and pale grey shirt and tie, the darkness of his hair curling silkily onto his shoulders. Much as he had looked the first morning they met. Just three days ago in actual time, but a lifetime away in the changes those same days had made within Nina.

And she wasn't just referring to the physical pleasure she had experienced with him last night.

These last few days with Rafe, and the things he had said to her last night when they argued, had made Nina once again question her own life, and the way in which she lived it.

Heaven knew, she never ever wanted to hurt her father. He had been hurt enough, but some of the things Rafe had said to her last night had settled deep within Nina, breaking open the fragile shell she had placed about her own hopes and dreams for the future, and forcing her to question as to whether or not, after all these years, it really was still necessary for her to live her life under the constant shadow of the past.

Surely there had to be some way of compromising? Some way of reassuring her father as to her safety, while at the same time being able to pursue her own dreams? Of being able to live her life without feeling as if she were in a gilded cage?

'It is not okay,' Rafe snarled as he spared a warning glare for the two burly bodyguards now flanking Nina. 'We're going up to my office to talk,' he rasped as he stood to one side to allow her to precede him out of the gallery.

Nina knew by the glitter in Rafe's eyes, his tight and thinned mouth, tensed jaw, and the angry flare of his nostrils that he was barely holding his temper in check.

A temper Nina hadn't even realised he possessed until this moment, Rafe's usual mood seeming to be one of laid-back charm and private amusement at the world.

Neither did Nina understand the reason for his current mood. The two of them had been out to dinner together yesterday evening, after which they had spent the night together, enjoyed each other to the full—as the pleasurable aches in Nina's body testified!—so what was Rafe's problem this morning?

Surely this was the way the game was played? No strings, no attachments, no expectations, on either side? Rafe's past history with relationships certainly said that was the way he liked to live his own life. And it was the way Nina had decided she would treat their relationship.

'I'm busy, Rafe.'

'Now, Nina!' he bit out harshly, a nerve pulsing in his tightly clenched jaw.

'I don't think you should be talking to Miss Palitov in that tone of voice, Mr D'Angelo.'

'Stay out of this!' Rafe turned fiercely on the bodyguard. Rich or Andy—they were interchangeable as far as he was concerned!

He was just relieved to have something else—someone else—to vent his frustrations on.

Rafe's imagination had run riot once he accepted that Nina had left his apartment without so much as saying goodbye. He wondered if in the clear light of day she was angry or upset about last night, or maybe a combination of the two.

He had become even more frustrated when he realised he didn't even have a personal telephone number on which he could contact her, and he had been in no mood to speak with her father to get to her, either. No doubt the older man would have been informed, and have an opinion, on where his daughter had spent the previous night.

Not that Rafe gave a damn how Dmitri Palitov felt about that. He just wanted to talk to Nina, and he was pretty sure, after the previous warning Dmitri had given him in respect of his daughter, that the older man wouldn't be in the least helpful in that regard.

Showering quickly before dressing and driving over to Nina's apartment hadn't been in the least productive either. The two men manning the reception desk—obviously yet more of the Palitov security—refused to tell Rafe anything other than Miss Palitov was 'currently not at home'.

An ambiguous answer that caused Rafe to question whether or not Nina really wasn't in her apartment, or just not at home to him, in particular?

Annoyed, frustrated, and more than a little concerned as to the reasons Nina had decided to leave so abruptly, and with no way of knowing and no one to answer those concerns, Rafe had driven to Archangel, deciding he would contact Nina again later today. Only to be told when he entered the gallery that Nina was here, as she had been for the past three days, working in the east gallery organising the display of the Palitov jewellery collection.

Rafe had gone straight to the east gallery, where he found Nina down on her hands and knees calmly arranging her father's jewellery collection in one of the display cases—as if last night hadn't happened. As if she hadn't left Rafe's apartment this morning before he had even woken up, as if he hadn't been worried as to why she might have done that! It had turned his churning emotions, his worry and concern, into a burning fury.

A fury that he realised was all the more deeply felt because he had opened up to this woman last night. Let his guard down, confided things in her, in a way he had never done with any other woman.

He was certainly in no mood to deal with her two overprotective, over-muscled security guards. 'We can have this conversation here, Nina, or we can have it upstairs in my office,' he bit out coldly. 'It's your choice.'

Nina wasn't at all reassured by the anger she could see blazing in Rafe's eyes. Although she was still puzzled as to the reason for it; she had thought he would be relieved when he woke up alone in his bed, that it was the way these things were done.

But she did accept that continuing this conversation in front of Rich and Andy wasn't a good idea. The two men looked ready to physically attack the other man, if they deemed it necessary. And that challenging glint in Rafe's eyes said he would welcome a show of the aggression.

'Fine.' Nina removed the thin cotton gloves she had worn for her work. 'You had better stay with the collection,' she instructed Rich and Andy. 'I'll only be a few minutes,' she assured them lightly.

'I wouldn't count on it,' Rafe muttered as she passed him in the doorway.

Nina gave him a frowning glance, her own anger stirring as Rafe continued to look grim as he fell into step beside her. Her anger deepened as he made no effort to explain himself, either outside in the hallway, or as they walked up the stairs to his office.

All of that changed the moment they had crossed through his assistant's office and closed Rafe's office door behind them. Nina suddenly found herself with her back pressed flush against that door, with Rafe towering over her, his hands either side of her head as he glowered down at her.

She frowned her displeasure as she felt imprisoned, both by Rafe's hands placed either side of her and pinning her in place, and his close proximity. A proximity that her traitorous body instantly reacted to by becoming achingly aroused, her nipples tightening into swollen, aching buds beneath her T-shirt, that familiar dampness gushing between her thighs.

'What's this all about, Rafe?' Her voice was sharp with irritation, at her physical response to him rather than Rafe's incomprehensible behaviour.

His eyes narrowed. 'You left.'

'What?'

'Why did you leave this morning, Nina?'

She gave a puzzled shake of her head. 'I don't understand the question.'

'Do I take it from your answer that you're in the habit of sneaking out of a man's apartment, without so much as a goodbye, after spending the night with him?' he grated harshly.

Nina's eyes flashed. 'I didn't sneak.'

'What the hell else would you call it?' Rafe snarled.

'I would call it your still being asleep when I woke up and my needing to get back to my own apartment to shower and change before coming in to work!' she snapped back dismissively.

'Without saying good morning or goodbye?'

She shrugged. 'As I said, you were asleep.'

'And we had just spent an incredible night together. You didn't consider waking me before you left?'

'No.' Her chin rose challengingly as she reminded him, 'You told me Michael would be arriving today.'

'This evening, not this morning,' he rasped impatiently. 'Besides which, I doubt my brother would go into shock at finding a woman in the apartment.'

'Probably not, no,' she drawled, sure that it was an occupational hazard for the three charismatic D'Angelo brothers, if they shared the same apartments around the world.

Not so much for Gabriel, of course, now that he was married, but Nina had no doubts that the brothers were used to stumbling across each other's lovers in the morning. Even the aloofly austere Michael, although no doubt more discreet about his relationships than his two younger brothers, was too charismatically handsome not to have a succession of women in his bed. That very austereness with which he surrounded himself was a challenge to any red-blooded woman.

'I would prefer it if he didn't find me there,' Nina added decisively.

Rafe looked down at Nina searchingly for several long seconds before pushing away from the door to move sharply away from her and stand in front of the window with his back towards the room. He thrust his clenched hands into the pockets of his trousers as he resisted the urge to grasp hold of her shoulders and shake her.

He was more than a little annoyed with himself because he wanted to kiss Nina again, make love to her again, rather than continuing with this less than satisfying conversation.

And it was playing havoc with his self-control that Nina still managed to look so damned fresh and alluring, despite the lack of sleep during the night of pleasure they had just spent together. Low-rise skinny black denims rested low on her hips, below a T-shirt the same green as her eyes. Her fiery red hair was caught up in a ponytail at her nape, her face appearing bare of make-up, and revealing those endearing freckles across the bridge of her nose.

Rafe, on the other hand, now had irritation to add to the blackness of his mood, the worry he had suffered after waking and finding Nina gone obviously completely unnecessary. 'Why did you leave, Nina?' he repeated harshly.

Nina frowned as she looked across the room at the stiffness of Rafe's back, her own anger at his behaviour now still burning low in her stomach. 'Is that what all this is about?' she questioned incredulously. 'Because I dared to leave Rafe D'Angelo's apartment this morning without his say-so?'

He turned abruptly, a dark scowl on his brow. 'You didn't need my permission to leave.'

'No?' Nina challenged, hands on her hips. 'That isn't the impression I'm getting right now!'

Those golden eyes narrowed. 'And what impression are you getting right now?'

She gave a scornful smile. 'That Rafe D'Angelo is usually the one who does the leaving. That it's all right for him to sneak out of a woman's apartment the morning after, but damned infuriating for a woman to dare to do the same thing to him!'

That there was some truth in her accusation didn't help Rafe's current mood of frustrated anger. Going to bed with a woman, spending part of the night with her in her apartment, had never been a problem for him, but he rarely—in fact, never!—stayed the whole night. He always left before he had to go through the awkward-ness of sitting across a breakfast table, trying to make conversation with the woman he had just had sex with.

Nina had been different. Not only was she the first

woman he had ever confided in, but she was also the first woman he had taken back to the family-owned apartment. He had actually been looking forward to making her breakfast, to talking and laughing with her as they shared that breakfast, in bed or out of it. Just as he had been anticipating how sexy she would look dressed only in one of his own shirts, before he carried her back to bed and made love with her again.

That he had never wanted that intimacy with another woman only made Nina's leaving all the more frustrating. Finding her calmly working at Archangel, as if nothing had happened between them last night, certainly hadn't improved his mood. Nevertheless…

'I never take women back to my apartment.'

She blinked. 'You don't?'

'No.'

'And yet you took me there?'

A nerve pulsed in his jaw. 'Yes.'

'Why?'

'At this moment I have absolutely no idea!' he rasped coldly.

'Oh.' Nina eyed him uncertainly.

'Yes,' he bit out succinctly.

She rallied determinedly. 'That's still no reason for you to have behaved like a Neanderthal downstairs!'

'A what?' Rafe prompted incredulously, eyes wide beneath his raised brows.

'A Neanderthal,' she repeated. 'Primitive man. As in "you woman, me man".'

'I know what it is, thank you,' Rafe drawled, some of his anger evaporating, to be replaced by amusement at hearing Nina accuse him of behaving like a caveman.

Which, with hindsight, he could see that he had done, and still was.

Just because Nina had walked out on him this morning? Or something else? Something more?

Nina had certainly got to him in a way no other woman had, but surely that didn't mean—

'Then why bother asking?' Nina snapped impatiently, hands thrust into the back pockets of those tight-fitting denims as she glared across the office at him, thrusting her breasts forward.

And instantly causing Rafe's body to throb and ache with the desire to make love to her all over again.

What was it about this woman, this woman in particular, that he had told her those things about himself last night? That he became aroused just looking at her flashing green eyes, those lushly full lips, the challenging tilt of that stubborn little chin, and those breasts tipped by hard little points visible against her T-shirt? Damned if Rafe knew, he only knew that he did.

He sighed heavily. 'Okay, so I might have come on a little strong downstairs.'

'A little strong?' Nina echoed scathingly as she began to pace the office like a caged tigress. 'You not only embarrassed yourself but you embarrassed me too.' She glared at him. 'Rich and Andy know exactly where I spent the night, an awkwardness I already have to deal with. I certainly didn't need you bursting into the gallery just now behaving like some prehistoric—'

'I think I got that part of the conversation,' Rafe drawled dryly.

'Then I suggest you make a note of it for any future relationships you might have,' she snapped. 'Because women have moved on a long way since we all lived in caves.'

His brows rose. 'I'm perfectly happy with the relationship I have at the moment, thanks very much.' And he wasn't sure he felt altogether comfortable discussing any future relationships with the woman he was currently involved with, either. The woman he had spent such an amazing night with. The woman he wanted to spend many more nights with.

'We don't have a relationship, Rafe,' Nina told him evenly.

'Last night—'

'Was last night,' she insisted firmly. 'And one night does not a relationship make,' she added decisively.

Rafe stilled as he eyed her guardedly. 'Then what does it make?'

Nina shrugged slender shoulders. 'It made for a few very enjoyable hours in bed together.' She deliberately used the past tense, knowing she would never forget those precious hours, at the same time as she accepted she had been just another conquest for Rafe, just another woman to fall for his charm.

But she had known that when she went to bed with him, so no recriminations there. It wasn't Rafe's fault that her emotions had become involved to a degree where Nina wasn't sure if she wasn't already half in love with him.

Rafe didn't care for the past tense in Nina's statement. 'And is that your usual modus operandi? Spend the night with a man and then just walk away?' he persisted, now wondering exactly what Nina had meant the previous evening when she had told him she 'lacked experience'? That inexperience certainly hadn't been apparent last night when the two of them had enjoyed each other so completely.

He'd assumed at the time that Nina had meant that she'd had a couple of previous lovers, but nothing serious; her offhand attitude towards him this morning, to the night the two of them had spent together, seemed to imply otherwise. And he didn't like it; he didn't like it at all.

Nina didn't like the sneer she could hear in Rafe's tone. At the same time she wasn't willing to back down on the stance she had decided to take where he was concerned.

Rafe might give the outward impression of a relaxed and charming playboy, but after their conversation last night Nina now knew there was another man behind that façade. A man of astute business acumen and deep intelligence. And curiosity.

And intelligence and curiosity were things she simply couldn't afford where her father and the past were concerned.

But that didn't stop her from wishing it could have been otherwise.

She had woken a little after six this morning, her body a pleasurable ache as she'd turned to find Rafe sleeping soundly beside her. She hadn't been able to resist lingering, for just a few minutes, in order to study him in the early morning sunlight streaming in through the windows.

His face had appeared almost boyish in his relaxed state, the overlong darkness of his hair a silky curtain about those relaxed patrician features. Long lashes a dark sweep above the sharpness of his cheekbones, chiselled lips curving in a smile even in his sleep.

The sheet had fallen down to his waist, leaving his bronzed and muscled chest bare. His chest was covered in that light dusting of ebony hair that formed a vee down to the flatness of his navel, and lower, to where his shaft already lay aroused against his stomach.

Rafe was, without a doubt, the most beautiful man Nina had ever seen.

And last night he had been all hers, to kiss and touch.

Their lovemaking was beyond anything Nina had ever imagined it could be, their bodies seeming to be totally attuned to pleasuring each other, each kiss, each caress a symphony of that pleasure.

It had been a beautiful night. One that Nina never intended to forget. But, as she had lain beside Rafe, drinking in her fill of him, she had known that it was over. That, for her father's sake, it had to be.

She certainly wasn't about to put her father at risk and become Rafe's 'sometimes' girl. She knew Rafe well enough, his history with women well enough, to know that, despite their closeness last night, he had no intentions of settling down with one woman.

She gave a dismissive smile. 'There's nothing worse than waking up the morning after and turning over and being sorry that the person beside you is there.'

Rafe drew in a hissing breath, his eyes as hard as the gold they resembled. 'And is that what happened to you? Did you wake up this morning and look at me and regret last night had ever happened?'

'Don't be silly, Rafe.' She forced a tinkling, dismissive laugh, knowing she would never, could never, regret waking up beside Rafe this morning. But if he wanted to think that was what she had done, then perhaps she should just leave him under that misapprehension.

'The two of us have a business relationship, and I think it's more important we continue to maintain that than pursuing any fleeting pleasure we might find in going to bed together for a few days or weeks.'

'A business relationship,' he echoed softly.

She nodded. 'There's my father's exhibition, and you asked me to consider designing some display cabinets for the Archangel galleries,' she reminded him.

'An offer I seem to remember you refused.'

Nina avoided meeting his piercing gaze. 'And which I'm now reconsidering. Unless you've changed your mind?'

'I haven't, no. But I'm curious as to why you've changed yours,' he prompted shrewdly.

It was a good question. And the simple answer to that lay in the decision she had made during the night regarding her future. No matter how much her father might fight against it, it really was time, past time, for her to start to break free of the confines that had been put on her life. Rafe's barbs had shown her she needed to start to make a life of her own.

And the best way Nina could think of to start doing that was to make that career for herself. Without the help of her father. And certainly without continuing to sleep with the man responsible for offering her the commission that would be the stepping stone to her starting that career.

The Archangel galleries, in New York, Paris and London, were the most prestigious privately owned galleries in the world, and having her work on show there, by designing display cases for each of the three galleries, would bring her work to the attention of collectors and other galleries.

'Why not, when it seems I already have my first commission?' she came back dismissively.

Rafe couldn't say he didn't feel a certain satisfaction in hearing Nina say she had finally decided to break away from her father, to do something she wanted to do. He just questioned the reasons as to why she was choosing to do it now.

He was also far from pleased at the way Nina so easily dismissed the idea of there being any future relationship between the two of them.

'If you feel it could be a problem for us after last night,' she continued lightly, 'then I can always discuss my ideas with Michael when I see him tomorrow evening.'

Rafe tensed as he felt a sharp pang of— Of what? Jealousy? He had never been jealous over a woman in his life!

His emotions had never been engaged enough in the past with any of the women he had been involved with to ever feel anything so basic as jealousy because of them.

Another way in which his feelings towards Nina were different from anything he had felt before?

His mouth thinned at the suggestion. He liked Nina, had very much enjoyed making love with her last night, but that was all he felt for her. He certainly wasn't jealous of her suggestion she spend time with Michael tomorrow night. 'It was my idea, my project, which means that Michael will also insist you deal directly with me, and not him.'

Nina's eyes widened at the harshness of Rafe's tone. She was unsure as to the reason for it. Any woman, unaware of Rafe's aversion to emotional entanglement, might have thought that he was expressing jealousy at her suggestion of talking with his haughty but equally handsome older brother. Because Rafe D'Angelo didn't do emotions like jealousy; why should he, when he could have any woman he wanted just by crooking his little finger at them?

No, Rafe was obviously still annoyed with her for having left his apartment this morning without saying goodbye. As annoyed, it seemed, as Nina was relieved that she'd found the strength to do so.

It would have been so much easier not to leave, to wake Rafe instead, to spend the morning in bed with him, making love with him. But she felt far too much for him already to allow herself to become any more deeply involved with him; she also knew she was just asking for her heart to be broken if she continued to be intimate with him.

If it wasn't already too late.

She had never met anyone like Rafe before. A man who had everything, it seemed. A successful business-man. Confident and wealthy and so handsome he made her heart beat faster just to look at him. So charming it took every effort of will on her part to resist giving him whatever he asked of her. So indulgent and experienced a lover that Nina had lost count of the amount of times she had climaxed in his arms last night.

Just so everything that Nina was afraid she might al-ready, stupidly, have fallen in love with him.

'Fine,' she accepted abruptly. 'Was that all? It's the gala opening tomorrow night, and I really need to get back to the gallery now and finish placing the jewellery in the cabinets.'

Rafe barely managed to bite back his irritation, his frustration, with this conversation. With Nina. With the fact that she had somehow managed to answer, and yet at the same time not answer, a single one of the ques-tions he had asked her.

Why had she left so abruptly this morning? Was that how she usually reacted after spending the night with a man? If she had been the one to wake up beside him this morning and regretted spending the night with him? And lastly, why had she chosen today, of all days, to decide to begin to break away from her father, to pursue her own career, by accepting Rafe's commission to design the display cabinets for the three Archangel galleries?

All of her answers to those questions had been either outright avoidance or glibness. Two behaviours Rafe had never before associated with Nina.

Two behaviours he found damned irritating, if he was honest with himself. Because they stopped him from reaching Nina. They erected a barrier between the two of them, and one that she seemed determined to keep firmly in place.

He sighed his frustration with the situation. 'Is there going to be any fall-out for you, with your father, because you stayed at my apartment last night?' he prompted impatiently.

Nina hadn't seen her father yet today, but she had no doubt he would know by now that she had spent the previous night at Rafe D'Angelo's apartment. Just as she had no doubts he would mention it to her when she saw him later this evening.

And Nina had absolutely no idea what he was going to say to her on the subject.

She was close enough to her father that she usually knew how he would react in any given situation, but her having stayed the night at Rafe's apartment was so unusual that Nina really had no idea what her father's opinion on that was going to be. No doubt she would find out later this evening.

'It's a little late to think about that, isn't it, Rafe?' she said dryly.

He shrugged. 'I'll talk to him if that would make it easier for you.'

Nina eyed him scathingly. 'And say what, exactly?'

'That it's none of his damned business where you spent the night.'

'No, thanks, I think I can handle it.' She chuckled wryly, recalling the phone conversation she'd had with her father the first time he realised she had been with a man. It had been embarrassing for them both, but that was all it had been; much as he wanted to protect her, to keep her safe, her father also wanted her to enjoy what other twenty-something women enjoyed. As long as it was in the circle of his protection.

'This isn't the first time it's happened, hmm?' Rafe rasped knowingly.

'Now you're being deliberately insulting again.' A frown creased Nina's brow as she looked across at him reprovingly.

'Am I?' He crossed the room in restless strides before sitting down in the chair behind his desk. 'Maybe that's because I'm finding the whole of our present conversation insulting. We spent an enjoyable evening together—apart from when I made you cry,' he acknowledged tightly. 'But we got over that, and spent an even better night together. And yet this morning you're telling me that you don't want to go out with me again, because you want to concentrate on your career.'

'I don't recall your having asked me to go out with you again,' Nina replied. 'But you're quite right in assuming my answer would have been no if you had,' she continued firmly as he would have spoken. 'We did have a lovely evening, and a fantastic night, and now it's time to get back to the real world.'

'And your real world doesn't have a place in it for me.' It was a statement rather than a question.

The only place Nina wanted Rafe in her life was one she could never have, nor was it one he was interested in her occupying. Despite the other side of Rafe she had discovered last night as they talked together, he had never pretended to be anything other than what he was: a thirty-four-year-old very eligible and handsome bachelor, who enjoyed women—lots of them.

Unfortunately Nina knew she wasn't made that way, which was why it was better, for both of them, if this ended now. And not just because of her father. She had to end this now, before she lost her pride, as well as her heart, to the point she was completely broken when Rafe ended their affair in a few weeks' time. As he surely would.

She raised her chin determinedly. 'Not at this point in time, no.'

He raised dark brows. 'And do you ever see a time when that might change?'

'No.'

'Fine,' Rafe rasped harshly. He wasn't about to beg, like a starving man asking for the scraps from Nina's table. If one night was all Nina wanted from him, then one night was all they would have.

All they'd had.

Because Nina had left him in no doubts that she considered the two of them to already be in the past tense.

CHAPTER EIGHT

'NOT GOING OUT this evening?'

Rafe turned to scowl at his older brother as Michael looked up at him from reading through the paperwork he had brought with him from Paris. He'd been working on it since he'd arrived at the apartment an hour or so ago.

'The clothes gave it away, huh?' Rafe scoffed. The faded denims and black T-shirt Rafe had changed into when he got back to the apartment that evening weren't something he would ever have worn to go out in on a Friday night.

'Somewhat,' Michael drawled. 'Rafe, will you stop pacing, damn it, and tell me what's wrong?' he added impatiently as Rafe continued to prowl restlessly around the sitting room.

Because Rafe felt too unsettled to join his brother by sitting down in one of the armchairs. As he had been too unsettled all day to be able to tackle any of the work piling up on his desk. How could he possibly concentrate on work when he knew that Nina was down in the east gallery, calmly arranging her father's jewellery collection in the display cabinets she had designed? And probably without so much as giving Rafe a second thought.

He had to admit, it was a little unusual for the woman to be the one to walk away from him. Unique, in fact.

And frustrating as hell, when Rafe was nowhere near to being ready to let Nina go.

She had been so damned cool this morning. So distant and in control as she'd told him their relationship—such as it was—was over.

Was that how he had appeared to all those women he had said goodbye to over the years? So cool and uninvolved emotionally as he told them he didn't want to see them again?

And had those women hated his guts in the same churning, furious, frustrated way that Rafe now—?

Now what?

Hated Nina?

Of course he didn't hate Nina. How could he possibly hate her when he still wanted her so damned much?

He was angry and frustrated, that was all, at having Nina end their relationship so abruptly. But it was his ego that had taken the knock, nothing else. And for no other reason than this had never happened to Rafe before, and he hadn't been ready to let Nina go, he assured himself.

'Rafe?'

He glanced across at Michael, knowing by his brother's perplexed frown that he really was concerned by his uncharacteristic distraction. 'It's nothing,' he dismissed impatiently. 'Do you want to order something in for dinner?' He moved to the desk to take out the menus for the restaurants he usually ordered food from the rare evenings he spent at home. The brothers' comings and goings were far too erratic for them to have ever considered taking on a full-time housekeeper.

Rafe wondered what Nina was doing for dinner this evening. No doubt she'd had some explaining to do to her father this evening. An explanation Rafe had half been expecting all day to have to make to Dmitri Palitov himself.

And Rafe readily admitted he had felt disappointed when the expected phone call from Dmitri, demanding an explanation from him, hadn't come. He had been spoiling for a fight with someone all day, and he would very much have enjoyed telling the older man to stay out of his own and Nina's business—endangering the exhibition of the unique Palitov jewellery collection, be damned!—as well as exactly what he thought of the older man for screwing up Nina's life.

Only to be left with a feeling of disappointment when he hadn't seen or heard from either member of the Palitov family all day.

'Rafe, what in the hell is wrong with you this evening?' Michael demanded impatiently.

'What?' Once again Rafe scowled his irritation as he turned back to his brother.

Michael put the paperwork aside. 'You've been holding those menus in your hands for the past five minutes, not looking at them, and not saying a damned word, just staring off into space.'

Yes, he had, Rafe realised self-disgustedly. 'So?' he challenged as he handed the menus to his brother.

'So it's the sort of taciturn behaviour I'd grown to expect from Gabriel pre-Bryn, but not from you.'

Rafe's mouth thinned. 'What docs that even mean?'

'It means you've been mooning about all evening.'

'I do not "moon about",' Rafe rasped scathingly. 'I'm just a little distracted, that's all.'

Michael's gaze sharpened. 'Are you having problems with the Palitov family?'

Rafe stiffened defensively, wondering how Michael

could possibly have known? Michael didn't know; he had to be referring to Dmitri Palitov rather than Nina Palitov.

'Not that I'm aware of, no,' he answered carefully; no doubt Dmitri Palitov would have something to say to him when the two men next met, but at this moment Dmitri hadn't told him how he felt in regard to the night Rafe had spent with his daughter.

Pure semantics, Rafe knew, because he could easily guess how the older man felt about it; he just didn't know for certain.

Michael nodded acceptance of his answer. 'Did you talk to the daughter?'

Rafe's tension increased. 'About what?'

'About your idea of commissioning the display cabinets for all the Archangel galleries from her, of course,' Michael answered impatiently. 'For God's sake, get a grip, Rafe. It was your recommendation that we ask her!'

Yes, it was, and it was a recommendation Rafe now had reason to regret. It very much looked as if Nina was going to accept the commission, and how the hell was he supposed to work on the design of those display cabinets with Nina when he only had to look at her to want her?

'She's on board with the idea.' He nodded. 'She said she would talk to you about it at the gala exhibition tomorrow night.' He bleakly recalled his own less than happy response to that suggestion.

A response that continued to fester and grow after Nina told him she didn't want to continue seeing him.

'Me?' Michael echoed blankly.

'Yes—you,' Rafe confirmed with hard derision. 'Obviously Miss Palitov considers, as you're the senior D'Angelo brother, that you're the one she should be talking to about this rather than your disreputable younger brother!'

'She doesn't realise that I'm the businessman in the family, Gabe's the artistic one, and you're the new ideas man for all the D'Angelo galleries?'

Rafe's mouth twisted. 'Does anybody?'

'And whose fault is that?' Michael frowned.

'Mine,' Rafe sighed. 'And it's never really bothered me before.'

'But it does now?'

It did, yes. Because for the first time in his life Rafe wanted someone, Nina, to see him not for who he was perceived to be but who he really was—the 'ideas man' of the D'Angelo family, as Michael had just called him.

Just earlier this evening the two brothers had discussed another new project of Rafe's that he had been thinking about the past few days, one in which they took Gabriel's original idea of a competition for new artists and broadened the spectrum to include all new artistic talent, from sculpture to the design of jewellery, giving over a room each month in the three galleries for displaying that talent.

The two previous competitions in the Paris and London galleries had been a great success, and a third was due to take place here in New York later in the year. Based on these successes, Rafe couldn't see any reason not to expand the idea.

It would mean a lot of hard work for each of the brothers, but Rafe believed the rewards, of discovering and exhibiting new artistic talent, would ultimately be well worth it. Instead of just selling or exhibiting great art, they would be discovering it.

Michael was already enthusiastic about the idea, and the two of them would discuss it with Gabriel once he was back from his honeymoon.

'Maybe,' Rafe conceded hardly.

'Becoming a little tired of the playboy label?'

'I believe I am, yes.' Especially so if it meant that was all Nina saw him as being!

'It's about time!'

'It is?' Rafe came back dryly.

His brother nodded. 'It was okay in your mid and late twenties, but it's good to see that it isn't enough for you now. You're a brilliant ideas man, Rafe, have always read the market perfectly, known in exactly which new direction we should take Archangel. I'd like other people to appreciate that as much as Gabe and I do. And I'll talk to Miss Palitov tomorrow evening, by all means.' Michael shrugged. 'But only to tell her that you're in charge of the project. As you're in charge of all new projects at Archangel.'

Oh, yes, Nina was going to learn that Rafe was very much 'in charge' when it came to anything to do with her, and anyone else, working within the realms of the Archangel galleries.

It might be sheer torture for Rafe to work with Nina, desiring her as he still did, but there was absolutely no way he was going to let her bypass him in favour of working with Michael.

Nina might not like it, but, as far as Rafe was concerned, if she was serious about wanting to design the new display cabinets for the three galleries, then she was stuck with him for the duration.

He looked across at his brother now. 'Ni— Someone made a comment to me a couple of days ago, implying that maybe the reason you've always had to be the serious one is because you had two mischievous younger brothers.'

Michael arched a dark brow. '"Someone"?'

'Someone,' Rafe insisted. 'Is it true?'

Michael gave the idea some thought. 'Maybe,' he finally conceded. 'As the eldest I always felt I had to be more responsible than you and Gabe.'

'Not much fun for you, though?'

'Has being the middle brother, feeling as if you have something to prove all the time, or constantly being the joker in order to grab your share of the attention, been any more fun?'

Rafe grimaced. 'Not really.'

Michael looked at him searchingly. 'You really are tired of that role, aren't you?'

Yes, he really was, and if he wasn't careful Michael was very soon going to ask why it was he suddenly felt that way. 'Let's order dinner, hmm?' he encouraged lightly, determined to change the subject and not to think about Nina, or anything she had said, again tonight.

Tomorrow night at the gala opening of her father's jewellery collection would be soon enough for that.

'If you have something to say, Papa, then I really wish you would just say it!' Nina frowned across at her father as the two of them travelled in the back of the limousine together on their way to the gala opening at the Archangel gallery on Saturday evening. The New York traffic was as dense and noisy as usual, the early evening sun shining into the smoked glass windows of the car through the gaps in the surrounding skyscrapers.

'About what, *maya doch*?' Her father returned her gaze steadily, his expression unreadable.

Nina gave a shake of her head. 'Don't be coy, Papa.'

He raised grey brows. 'In what way am I being coy?'

She sighed. 'You haven't said anything, but let's neither of us pretend you don't know about my having spent Thursday night at Rafe D'Angelo's apartment.'

It was a statement rather than a question. After all, she had been waiting thirty-six excruciating hours for her father to so much as mention the subject of her having spent the night with Rafe.

Her father shrugged. 'That is your affair, no?'

Her eyes widened. 'The other evening you warned him to stay away from me,' she reminded.

'Ah, he told you about that.' Her father nodded ruefully.

'Oh, yes,' she recalled with feeling.

'He was not pleased by my warning.' Her father nodded. 'As I fully expected he would not be.'

'And you knew I wouldn't like it either, so why do it?' Nina frowned.

'To see how Rafe would respond, of course,' he answered with satisfaction.

She stared at her father incredulously. 'You were testing him?'

'I was attempting to see what manner of man he is, yes,' her father acknowledged unapologetically.

'And?'

Dmitri gave a half-smile. 'And by inviting you out to dinner, spending the night with you, despite that warning, he has obviously shown himself to be a man who is not cowed, by me, or the Palitov name.'

Knowing Rafe, as she now did, Nina knew he was a man who wouldn't be cowed by much at all, least of all her father or the Palitov name.

And, much as she loved her father and didn't want to hurt him, she knew it was time for her to do the same.

She drew in a determined breath. 'Rafe approves of the display cabinets I designed for your collection, so much so he's asked me if I would design more for all the Archangel galleries,' she revealed huskily.

Unreadable emotion flickered in her father's eyes before it was quickly masked. 'And you wish to do this?'

Nina sat back as she met those guarded eyes a paler green than her own. 'I do, yes.'

'You now like him.' It was a statement rather than a question.

'Enough to spend the night with him, at least!'

'Perhaps we should discuss this further once we have returned home later this evening?' her father suggested as the limousine pulled up at the back of the Archangel gallery.

Her father had expressed a wish to be lifted from the car and into his wheelchair there, rather than in the full glare of the photographers crowded about the front steps of the gallery, eagerly snapping photographs for tomorrow's newspapers of the glittering array of personalities invited to attend this private showing of the Palitov jewellery collection.

'There is much I <u>still need</u> to tell you. About the past, *maya doch*,' he continued huskily. 'But this is not the place or time in which to do it.'

Nina gave her father a searching glance, noting the pained expression in his pale green eyes, the lines of tension beside his nose and mouth, the pallor of his hollowed cheeks. 'Are you quite well, Papa?' She placed a hand on his arm, feeling the way it trembled slightly beneath her fingertips. 'If you're unwell we don't have to attend the gala.'

'I am as well as I can ever expect to be in regard to my health, daughter,' he assured gruffly. 'My heart and mind are another matter, however. Not now, Nina.' He placed his hand over hers and squeezed lightly as he saw her anxious expression. 'We will attend and enjoy the gala together, as planned, and talk of these things again later tonight. I only hope you will be able to forgive me—' He broke off, his expression anguished as he looked across at her.

'Forgive you for what, Papa?' she prompted, fearing his anxiety had something to do with the fate of the three kidnappers.

'We will talk later,' he repeated determinedly.

She would have to be satisfied with that answer, for the moment.

Except she wasn't.

There had been something in her father's eyes just now, a darkness that spoke of pain, a deep-rooted pain he had never revealed to her before. But not of a physical kind, as he had assured her it wasn't, but one that bit deep into his heart and mind.

Not that Nina had any more time to think about that right now, when she had the ordeal of the gala exhibition at Archangel, and seeing Rafe again, to get through…

'I don't recall her being quite so beautiful.'

Rafe was only half listening to Michael, far too busy studying Nina as she arrived with her father. He was too busy looking for any signs in her expression that she found this evening as much of a strain as he did to give his brother his full attention.

Her eyes were that clear unshadowed green, her skin glowing with health and vitality, and she smiled brightly as her father introduced her to the two men who had just joined them, all of the guests having been waiting in anticipation for the arrival of the reclusive Dmitri Palitov.

Rather than strained Nina looked sensational. Absolutely, breathtakingly, sensational.

She had left her hair loose again tonight, a moving river of flame as it fell silkily over her shoulders before cascading down the length of her spine to her waist. Her emerald-green eyes dominated the creaminess of her face, and there was a deep rose gloss on those temptingly pouting lips. Her gown was a gold shimmer that clung lovingly to her curves, leaving her arms bare, and finishing several inches above her knees to reveal those long and shapely legs, her four-inch-heeled shoes the same rich gold colour as her gown.

And Rafe hadn't been able to take his eyes off her since the moment she had appeared in the doorway of the gallery beside her father's wheelchair, his eyes narrowing now as she laughed huskily at something said to her by one of the two men her father had introduced her to.

'Rafe, are you listening to me? Rafe!'

'What is your problem now, Michael?' He turned on his brother fiercely, his hands clenched into fists at his sides.

Michael raised calm dark brows at that show of aggression. 'I merely remarked on the fact that I don't remember Nina Palitov being quite so young or so beautiful. A remark which you obviously didn't hear. Or just didn't want to comment on,' he added shrewdly.

Rafe's scowl deepened. 'If you recall, I did mention the little fact of her beauty in my telephone call to you after I'd met Nina for the first time, after I had discovered she wasn't the middle-aged spinster you'd allowed me to expect!'

Michael grimaced. 'I didn't "allow" anything. I just wasn't taking a lot of notice of how the daughter looked when I last met Dmitri Palitov. But I'd have to be dead not to have noticed now.'

Rafe's eyes narrowed. 'What's that supposed to mean?'

His brother's gaze was still on the beautiful Nina as she stood beside Dmitri Palitov, so he didn't see the displeasure on Rafe's face. 'We should go over and greet our guest of honour,' he added distractedly.

Rafe placed a warning hand on his brother's arm. 'Keep your restrained but lethal charm to yourself around Nina!' he warned harshly.

Michael turned back to look at him, narrowed gaze raking slowly over Rafe's face. 'What the hell?' he finally muttered softly. 'Rafe, please tell me you didn't— Oh, hell, you did.' He grimaced as Rafe quirked one dark, pointed brow. 'I asked you to keep Dmitri Palitov sweet and you slept with his daughter!'

'Keep your damned voice down.' Rafe glared at him.

Michael continued to scowl at him. 'Is Nina Palitov the reason for your distraction yesterday evening? The reason you've been walking around growling at everyone at the gallery today? More to the point...' his brow slowly cleared '...is she the reason you've suddenly tired of the playboy image and decided it has to go?' he probed shrewdly.

'Mind your own damned—'

'It is my business, Rafe,' his brother cut in coldly. 'Anything that affects Archangel is my business. And Gabriel's too.'

'This has nothing to do with Archangel.'

'And what is "this", precisely?' Michael bit out softly. 'What does Nina Palitov mean to you?'

'None of your damned business.'

Michael gave an impatient sigh. 'Does Palitov know about the two of you?'

'There's nothing to know.'

'Does he know?' Michael grated harshly.

Rafe's jaw clenched. 'Yes. But it's already over between the two of us.'

'Why?' Michael's brows rose.

'Shouldn't you just be pleased that it is rather than asking why it is?'

'Not if it's not what you want, no.'

Rafe's brow cleared. 'You know, Michael, you really do live behind a mask as much as I do.'

'Meaning?'

'Meaning that you hide your emotions behind that mask. Meaning that maybe our little brother getting married has got to you.'

'As it's got to you?'

Nina was what had 'got to' Rafe. Just Nina. And he still had no idea what he was going to do about it. About her.

'Do you think he's just lulling you into a false sense of security by showing up here this evening?' Michael was staring across at Dmitri Palitov. 'And that maybe he intends to set some of his bodyguards on you in a dark alley one night?'

'I don't know how I've survived all these years without a daily dose of your sunny disposition.' Some of Rafe's own normal good humour returned. 'Let's go and say hello to them—and perhaps later you could let me know if you still think he intends having me discreetly eliminated.' He didn't wait to see what else his brother had to say on the subject as he made his way through the crowded gallery to where Nina stood beside Dmitri's wheelchair as Dmitri now chatted with several business acquaintances.

Nina found it slightly intimidating to have not one, but two, of the formidably handsome D'Angelo brothers bearing down on her. Or, to be strictly accurate, one of them was bearing down on her in that intimidating way; Michael D'Angelo's attention was obviously more focused on her father.

But the D'Angelo brothers were without doubt the two most arrestingly handsome men here this evening, their perfectly tailored black evenings suits and snowy white shirts emphasising the width of their muscled shoulders and the lean strength of perfectly toned bodies. Rafe's hair was a silky ebony curtain onto his shoulders, Michael's hair as dark but styled much shorter, and revealing stark and arresting features dominated by obsidian-black eyes.

And she was deliberately delaying looking at Rafe by keeping her gaze fixed firmly on his austerely handsome older brother.

She knew she had good cause for that delay when she finally turned the coolness of her gaze on Rafe and saw the angry glitter in those predatory gold eyes, and a nerve pulsing in his tensely clenched jaw.

Predatory golden eyes that held Nina's gaze captive as she distractedly acknowledged Michael D'Angelo's formally polite greeting before he turned to shake her father's hand with warmer familiarity. Rafe remained noticeably silent as he continued to look down at her with that piercing coldness.

What on earth was wrong with him? Admittedly the two of them had parted badly yesterday morning in his office, and they hadn't spoken a single word to each other since, but did Rafe have to make the tension that now existed between the two of them so obvious to other people? To her father? To his brother?

His next actions would seem to confirm that he did.

'If you will excuse us, gentleman, I just need to steal Nina from you for a few minutes,' Rafe rasped determinedly, not waiting for either man to respond as he reached out and circled one of Nina's wrists with steely fingers before he turned and walked in the direction of the gallery doorway.

Nina stumbled along beside him as she found it difficult to keep her balance in her four-inch-heeled shoes.

'You're making a scene again, Rafe!' she hissed as she saw the curious glances being sent their way.

His eyes glittered dangerously as he spared her the briefest of glances. 'Maybe you would rather I caused even more of a scene by pushing you up against the wall right here and taking you in front of everyone?'

'Rafe!' Nina wasn't sure whether her breathless gasping of his name was in shocked outrage or aching longing for him to do just that.

She had a sinking feeling it was the latter.

CHAPTER NINE

THE NEED TO kiss Nina again, to touch her and to make love to her again had been like a burning ache inside Rafe for the past thirty-six hours. He'd been kept in a state of arousal for almost all of that time too, until something had snapped inside him just now, just from looking at the way that clinging, glittering gold gown clung so lovingly to every curve of her delicious body, with her hair tumbling like a living flame over her shoulders and down the length of her spine. As for those lushly pouting lips…

'Don't even think about it,' he tensely instructed the two Palitov bodyguards on duty just outside the gallery as they stepped forward at first sight of Nina.

'It's okay, Andy,' Nina added ruefully as the larger of the two burly men turned to her enquiringly. 'Stay with my father. Mr D'Angelo and I are going for a little walk,' she added lightly as Rafe continued to pull her down the hallway.

Walk, be damned. Rafe needed to taste Nina again, to touch her again so badly, that he opened the first door he came to once they had turned the corner into another hallway, uncaring that it appeared to be some sort of small service cupboard containing brooms and buckets. He pushed her unceremoniously inside before following her in and shutting the door behind them, immediately throwing them into complete darkness.

'Rafe!'

'I need to kiss you, Nina!' he groaned as he lowered his head and fiercely captured her mouth unerringly with his, moaning his satisfaction at the first delicious taste of her.

All of Nina's annoyance at Rafe's high-handed behaviour in having dragged her from the gallery—very much in the manner of that Neanderthal she had accused him of being yesterday morning!—evaporated as if it had never been at the first touch of Rafe's mouth against hers. Her own desire for him was instantaneous, combustible.

Her lips parted beneath his, and she let her clutch bag slide to the floor before moving her arms up and over his shoulders to allow her fingers to become entangled in the darkness of Rafe's hair. She pressed the length of her body against his and returned the hunger of that kiss, her breasts swelling, nipples pebbling, between her thighs heating, as Rafe's hands roamed restlessly along the length of her spine before cupping her bottom and pulling her heat in tight against the hardness of his arousal.

He wrenched his mouth from hers, his hand fisting in her hair as he pulled back slightly, arching her neck to allow his lips and tongue to seek out the silky hollows and dips of her throat. 'Your father isn't going to be happy about this.' he acknowledged unconcernedly, his breath hot as his tongue rasped moistly against her skin, tasting her, drinking her in.

Nina gave a soft, breathless laugh. 'I'm not sure my father has any place here.'

'Hell, I hope not,' he muttered distractedly, his body throbbing with heat as he pressed into her more intimately still, moving his hips in a slow arousing rhythm, pressed up between the dampness of her thighs, even as one of his hands slipped beneath the hem of her gown to caress the length of her thigh. 'I need to feel your heat against my fingers, Nina.' He groaned as his fingers lingered at the lacy edge of her panties.

'Rafe!' Heat suffused the whole of her body in anticipation of her own need for the pleasure promised by those questing fingers.

'Are you wearing panties beneath this gown?'

'Yes,' Nina answered uncertainly.

'Minuscule ones, I'm guessing?'

'Very,' she confirmed dryly.

Rafe breathed deeply. 'And I just want to rip them off you, stroke and caress you and feel you as you climax! Then I want to lick my fingers and taste—'

'Rafe, please…' Nina groaned helplessly, unsure if she was pleading for him to stop or continue as just his words caused a gush of that hot moisture between her thighs.

'Oh, I want to please you, Nina,' he assured gruffly. 'I want that more than I want my next breath.'

Nina wanted it too. It didn't matter that they were squashed into what had looked like a cleaning storeroom before the door had closed and plunged them both into darkness. Nor was it important that just metres away from this small room there were two hundred people attending the jewellery exhibition, including her own father, all of whom had seen Rafe drag her out of the gallery just minutes ago.

All that mattered at this moment was being with Rafe, making love with Rafe, having Rafe kiss and caress her.

'Do it, Rafe,' she encouraged achingly, needily. 'Just do it!'

The words had barely left her lips when she heard the

delicate sound of lace and silk ripping as Rafe caught the side of her panties and pulled, a rustle of movement telling her that he had disposed of the ripped panties.

'You're so beautiful here,' Rafe murmured gruffly as he parted and then stroked the silky bareness of the flesh between her thighs, his face buried against her perfumed throat. 'So, so beautiful,' he groaned.

He began a gentle, teasing stroking, able to feel the way those swollen folds parted greedily with each measured caress. Nina's clitoris pulsing, swelling, as he pressed harder, caressed faster, before thrusting one, and then two fingers inside the heat of her, his fingers curling as he found that sensitive spot inside her. His thumb continued that sweet caress as she began to buck into those thrusts. Rafe's other arm tightened about Nina's waist as he felt those inner contractions deepen, lengthen, as her legs began to tremble and threatened to buckle beneath her.

'Yes, Nina,' Rafe encouraged hoarsely as he felt her climax hit with the force of a tsunami. 'I want it all, damn it. Give me every last measure of your pleasure,' he pressured fiercely.

Nina cried out as that pleasure ripped through her body in ever-increasing waves, her nipples hard and aching pebbles, her core tightening, grasping greedily at those thrusting fingers as they filled her time and time again. She felt completely boneless, incapable of standing, by the time the last wave of her climax had rippled through her. She would have collapsed down onto the floor if Rafe hadn't continued to hold her up with his arm about her waist.

Nina groaned, another wave of pleasure rippling through her as Rafe slowly eased his fingers out from the heat of her.

'Mmm, delicious,' he murmured appreciatively seconds later.

'What?'

'You taste like honey, Nina.'

'God…!' She rested the dampness of her forehead against the shoulder of his jacket, her cheeks burning at the thought of the intimacy of having Rafe licking his fingers, of his tasting her.

'The name's Rafe,' he came back with teasing softness as both his arms moved about her now.

'Egotist!' She gave his other shoulder a half-hearted punch. She simply didn't have the strength left to do any more than that. Her body was one big pleasurable ache. 'No doubt you're feeling almighty and powerful now.'

He chuckled huskily. 'No doubt.'

'You could try a little harder for modesty, Rafe,' she admonished ruefully.

'Not while I'm holding my very satisfied woman in my arms, I couldn't,' he drawled lightly.

His satisfied woman?

What did that even mean? Rafe had made it obvious that relationships weren't for him, that fun was his only aim, and that when the fun was over it was time to say goodbye.

Nina's life was too complicated to ever be thought of as fun.

She knew she should be feeling indignant at this further display of Rafe's arrogance, knew that she should pull out of his arms and tell him that this changed nothing between them. That she was determined to keep to her decision not to become any more involved with him. That she would never be any man's woman.

Except she couldn't do it. She didn't have the strength

right now to stand up unaided, let alone walk away from Rafe for a second time in as many days.

Later, she told herself. She would make him understand later.

'Come to my apartment tonight,' Rafe instructed gruffly—seeming to have picked up on some of her thoughts, at least. 'This should all be over by eleven o'clock. Spend the night with me, Nina, please,' he urged.

'What about Michael?' she questioned huskily.

'Michael can get his own woman.'

'I meant—'

'I know what you meant, darling Nina,' Rafe drawled indulgently. 'And the apartment is big enough that he doesn't even have to know you're there.'

Could she do that? Was it possible? Could she take, steal, another night in Rafe's arms, in his bed?

How could she refuse when he had given her such pleasure just now and taken nothing for himself? Her past experiences might not have been good ones, but she had never been a selfish lover.

'Because you want to, Nina, not because you feel obligated to give something back to me because of what happened just now.' This time Rafe seemed to pick up on all of her thoughts.

At the same time as he had managed to strip away all of the arguments Nina had been giving in order to justify to herself going to his apartment later tonight.

She moistened her lips before speaking. 'I think the more immediate problem is how are we going to walk out of this closet and go back into the gallery, having left together so abruptly a few minutes ago, without everyone knowing exactly what we've been doing?'

Rafe gave another chuckle. 'There's little chance of that happening. I happen to know exactly what you look like after pleasure, Nina, and believe me the hot, sultry glitter in your eyes, the blush in your cheeks, and those roused and puffy lips are a dead giveaway as to exactly what we've been doing.'

'Oh, very attractive,' she muttered. 'You make me sound like a wild woman.'

'No, just my woman.' His arms tightened about her. 'And I like you wild. I like it a lot.'

Nina liked the way Rafe made her feel wild too. A lot. Too much so to have the strength to deny herself just one more night in his arms.

'Even so, I think you should return to the gallery on your own now, and then I'll come back in a few minutes, when I've had a chance to tidy my appearance.'

'That's not going to change the fact that I will be aware for the rest of the evening that your ripped panties are sitting in my jacket pocket.'

Her cheeks felt warm at the knowledge that she was now completely naked beneath her gown, a gown that moved silkily, sensuously against the heat of her skin, and that it would also ensure she was aware of that fact for the rest of the evening.

'Okay, I'll come to your apartment later— Damn, I forgot! I have to go home with my father first,' she realised with a wince. 'We started a conversation on the way over here which we have to finish tonight,' she explained ruefully.

'Anything serious?' Rafe murmured softly, not completely happy with Nina's answer, but willing to settle for what he could get for the moment. He had seduced her once, he would do it again, and again, if necessary.

'I'm not sure,' Nina acknowledged slowly.

He frowned. 'Does it have anything to do with your

staying with me on Thursday night? Because if it does maybe I should—'

'No,' she assured him firmly. 'This is just something my father needs to discuss with me. But hopefully it won't take too long,' she assured lightly, 'and I can be with you before midnight.'

Rafe nuzzled his lips against the warmth of her throat. 'I'll see what I can do about persuading Michael into going straight to bed when we get home. Maybe remind him of his jet lag along with his advancing years.'

'He's only a year older than you are!'

'Only in calendar months. Still he wasn't particularly happy with me before I dragged you off into my cave,' Rafe mused ruefully.

'Why?' Nina prompted slowly.

'Because I told him about us.' He shrugged. 'Because he has the idea that your father might arrange to have me disposed of in a dark alley one night.'

Nina moved back slightly in his arms. 'My father isn't some sort of gangster, Rafe.'

He chuckled as his arms tightened about her. 'I never said he was.'

'But you and Michael think of him as being one?'

'Hey.' Rafe sobered as he heard the strain in Nina's voice. 'It was just Michael's idea of a joke, Nina.'

'If you thought that about him, I'm surprised either of you wanted to risk sullying the name of Archangel by displaying my father's jewellery collection,' she came back sharply. 'After all, he might have stolen some, if not all, of it.'

'Nina, don't—' He broke off as she pulled completely out of his arms. 'Nina?'

'We should get back.'

'Not like this,' Rafe groaned in protest at the distance

he could feel yawning between them again, Nina refusing to allow him to take her back into his arms. 'I didn't mean to upset you just now, Nina. My remark really was meant as a joke. Obviously it was in poor taste,' he added regretfully.

Unfortunately, Nina's suspicions in regard to her father's accident nineteen years ago prevented her from seeing anything in the least humorous in Rafe and Michael's comments about her father.

'I really have to go, Rafe.' She opened the door before bending down to pick up her clutch bag from where she had allowed it to fall to the floor earlier, only to straighten and find herself prevented from leaving because Rafe had moved to stand in the doorway in front of her.

Allowing her to see now that the darkness of his hair was slightly tousled from where her fingers had been enmeshed in it just minutes ago, but otherwise Rafe looked as handsome and impeccable in his appearance as he had before their little sojourn to the supply cupboard.

Whereas Nina was pretty sure her own appearance was one of total dishevelment, and that she definitely looked like a woman who had just been made love to fully and well.

And there was no denying that feeling of satisfied heaviness between her thighs, or the fact that she was fully aware of the fact that she now wore no panties beneath her short and clinging gown!

'You'll still come to me later?' Rafe looked down at her searchingly.

She really should say no. Should keep to the decision she had made yesterday morning, not to see or be with Rafe again, and so give him the opportunity to probe and push into the past.

That was what she should do.

Unfortunately, that ache in her body said otherwise. 'I'll still come to your apartment later,' she confirmed huskily.

'Good.' He nodded his satisfaction with her reply. 'I suppose you're right, and we have to go back to the exhibition now.' He grimaced.

Nina had to smile at his obvious lack of enthusiasm for the idea. A lack of enthusiasm she echoed.

'Nina?' The hand Rafe placed lightly on her arm halted her as they stepped out into the hallway together.

She glanced up at him warily. 'Yes?'

His hands moved up to cup either side of her face, his gaze holding hers captive as he slowly lowered his head to brush his lips lightly against hers. 'Thank you,' he murmured huskily.

Nina's heart beat a wild tattoo in her chest at the touch of his lips and his close proximity. 'For what?' she breathed softly.

'Just thank you.' Rafe wasn't a hundred per cent sure himself what he was thanking Nina for.

Maybe for not slapping him in the face earlier, when he had dragged her out of the gallery like the caveman she had accused him of being yesterday?

Or perhaps because, once they were alone together, she hadn't even attempted to deny the attraction that still burned so fiercely between the two of them?

Or maybe because of the pleasure her uninhibited response gave him. Rafe was certainly no longer suffering with that same frustrated anger he had been plagued with for the past thirty-six hours.

Or maybe he was thanking her for simply being Nina?

Rafe had the rest of the evening to get through before he could even begin to give that revelation any deeper thought.

* * *

'Are you sure you're quite well, Papa?' Nina prompted concernedly as she saw how pale her father was looking when she rejoined him in the gallery. She hoped that his pallor was due to the effort of socialising, after so many years of avoiding it, rather than her own disappearance with Rafe just a short time ago.

She had done what she could to tidy her appearance once she reached the ladies' room, but brushing her hair and reapplying lip gloss had done nothing to hide that sultry glow Rafe said she had after lovemaking. A glow that had noticeably darkened her eyes to deep emerald, rendered her cheeks a delicate peach, and left her lips plump and rosy from Rafe's kisses.

'I am quite well, *maya doch*,' her father assured as he looked up at her searchingly. 'You and Rafe D'Angelo are...friends again?'

'I wasn't aware we were ever anything else.' Nina avoided meeting her father's probing gaze as she blushed.

'I believe we have passed the stage of coyness in regard to your relationship with D'Angelo, Nina,' he reproved softly.

There was every reason for Nina to blush, when she could so clearly remember the wildness, the heat, of the lovemaking between her and Rafe such a short time ago.

It was as if they had been starved for each other, wild with need.

Rafe compelled to touch her and Nina desperate to feel his touch. She had been completely aware of the heat still throbbing between her bare thighs as she crossed the gallery to rejoin her father.

She glanced across to where Rafe stood in conversation with his brother, just in time to see him put his hand in the pocket of his jacket where he had placed those ripped panties.

As if he sensed her glance Rafe's gaze rose to meet hers, those predatory golden eyes glittering with memories, chiselled lips slowly curving into a smile that was a promise of yet more pleasure to come when she joined him at his apartment later.

'You're pacing again.'

Rafe shot a malevolent glare across the kitchen to where Michael sat at the breakfast bar enjoying his morning tea and toast as he read the business section in the Sunday newspaper.

And of course Rafe was pacing, damn it, because Nina hadn't turned up at the apartment last night as she had said she would.

He and Michael had arrived back at a little before midnight the previous evening, Michael needing no persuading in taking himself off to bed—perhaps because he had guessed that Rafe was expecting Nina to join him?

Rafe had waited for Nina to arrive until one o'clock before phoning down to the security desk on the ground floor, to see if he had somehow missed her, only to be told that there had been no visitors for him at all that evening.

Rafe had waited another hour before telephoning security again. Only to be given the same answer.

At which time he had realised Nina wasn't going to come to him tonight, after all.

But even then, remembering the seriousness of her tone when she had mentioned the conversation she needed to have with her father before she could join him at his apartment, Rafe had been more worried than annoyed. He didn't at all like the possibility of Nina being upset and alone in her own apartment.

Although a call from her, telling him of her change of plans, might have been nice.

Even so, worry niggled at Rafe, until in desperation he had called her apartment building, asking the security guard on duty to put him through to Nina's apartment, only to discover that she wasn't in her apartment to answer his call. Nor would the security guard on the other end of the line reveal whether or not she had returned to the building with her father earlier, or whether or not she had gone out again.

And there was no way Rafe was going to call Dmitri's apartment and ask him where his daughter was.

Instead Rafe had finally gone to bed. Alone. But not to sleep.

Because, no matter how much he punched and pummelled his pillows to get comfortable, sleep had eluded him. Rafe simply lay in the bed, wide-eyed, his brain working overtime as he went over and over the events of the rest of yesterday evening, trying to find some reason, something he might have done or said, to make Nina change her mind about spending the night with him.

The only thing he knew she had taken exception to was that remark he had made about her father, but even that didn't make sense, because Nina had confirmed that she would come to his apartment after Rafe had made that foolish joke.

Which was the reason it was now ten o'clock on a Sunday morning, and he was pacing up and down the kitchen on bare feet, still wearing the black T-shirt and grey sweats he had slept in, his hair standing on end from where he had run his fingers through it so often in the past ten hours, while at the same time suffering Michael's penetrating and knowing gaze.

'I fully expected to see Nina here with you this morning,' Michael prompted softly.

'Well, obviously you expected wrong!' Rafe scowled at him darkly.

Michael nodded. 'Obviously. Rafe—' He broke off as the telephone rang.

Rafe crossed the kitchen quickly to snatch up the receiver, hoping—praying—it was Nina. 'Yes?' he snapped impatiently.

'There's a visitor waiting down in Reception to see you, Mr D'Angelo,' Jeffrey, the doorman informed, sounding slightly nervous.

'Send her right up,' Rafe barked sharply.

'But—'

'Now, Jeffrey.' Rafe slammed down the receiver, his pacing restless now rather than angry, as he waited impatiently for Nina to ring the doorbell.

'I think I'll go shower and dress ready for leaving for the airport shortly—' Michael rose to his feet '—and leave you two alone to talk and sort out whatever it is you need to.'

'Thanks,' Rafe answered distractedly, barely aware of his brother leaving as he strode out into the hallway to wait for Nina.

Whatever the reason for Nina's no show last night, she was here now, and that was all that mattered.

The doorbell had hardly finished ringing when Rafe threw open the door, the welcoming smile freezing on his lips as he saw the two burly bodyguards standing shoulder to shoulder outside in the hallway, their eyes once again hidden behind those wrap-around sunglasses. That probably explained Jeffrey's nervousness on the telephone just now.

Rafe couldn't say he was particularly happy at seeing the two bodyguards either. 'What—?'

'I'm sorry for the intrusion, Rafe.' The two body-guards had parted to reveal Dmitri Palitov sitting in his wheelchair in the hallway behind them. 'I wondered, if my daughter is here with you, if I might speak with her?' His expression was hopeful rather than condemning.

That told Rafe that Dmitri Palitov had no more idea where Nina was than he did.

CHAPTER TEN

NINA HELD HER head confidently high as she walked into the Archangel gallery late on Monday morning, her smile conveying that same confidence to the receptionist, in her right to be here, as the other woman nodded in recognition as Nina walked towards the staircase that would take her up to Rafe's office on the third floor of the building.

Rafe…

Nina had no doubt that he was going to be far from happy with her, for not having turned up at his apartment on Saturday night, and for not getting in touch with him since then to explain why she hadn't.

Rafe might have claimed to have been joking on Saturday evening, as to the possibility of her father being some sort of gangster, but Nina had always had her own suspicions that weren't so far from the truth. Her conversation with her father late on Saturday evening hadn't gone far enough to confirm that, but it had certainly proved to her how powerful a man her father really was.

As a result, Nina knew there was no way she could ever tell Rafe of those new and shocking truths about her mother that her father had revealed to her late Saturday evening. Nina was having trouble accepting that truth herself, so how could anyone else possibly be expected to understand?

Which was why Nina had decided—again!—that from now she and Rafe could only have a business relationship. She would design the new display cabinets for the Archangel galleries, and as one of the owners of those galleries Rafe could approve those designs. Straightforward. Simple.

At least, it had seemed straightforward and simple when Nina had made that decision in her hotel room yesterday. She'd spent most of the night sitting dry-eyed in a chair beside the window looking sightlessly out at the New York skyline, wondering how, after the things her father had told her about her mother, she was going to get through the next few hours, let alone all the days that were to follow.

Here and now, with Rafe just a staircase away, her decision seemed far from simple. Rafe had already shown that he wasn't the type of man to just accept what she said at face value, that he would want to prod and probe in order to learn the reasons for her having made that decision. Reasons Nina couldn't possibly share with him. That she couldn't share with anyone.

Her footsteps slowed, grew heavier, the closer she got to Rafe's office. To the confrontation she had decided she had no choice but to face if she really was serious in her intention to make a life for herself. She planned to start by setting up her own business, well away from her father's influence. This work for the Archangel galleries was her door into doing that, at least.

All she had to do, before any of that became possible, was to fend off or dismiss any of Rafe's demands for the answers she couldn't give him.

All she had to do!

Just standing here outside the door to Rafe's office

made her heart pound louder and her palms grow damp, so how much worse was it going to be once she was face to face with him?

'Bridget, I thought I told you no interruptions—Nina!' Rafe rasped in recognition as he looked up from the catalogue he had been studying and saw it was Nina standing in the doorway rather than his assistant.

He stood up to move swiftly around his desk and cross the room in long strides before taking one of her hands in both of his, his gaze roaming over her face searchingly—hungrily!—easily noting the pallor of her cheeks and the distance in those cool green eyes that looked into his so steadily.

'Have I come at a bad time?' Her voice had that same distance and coolness.

He continued to look at her searchingly, wanting, needing to see some of 'his Nina' in the pained depths of her eyes. 'Are you okay?' Stupid question, Rafe instantly rebuked himself impatiently; of course Nina wasn't okay!

If Nina was 'okay' she wouldn't have walked out of her father's apartment on Saturday night. If she was 'okay' she would have come to Rafe that same night, as they had agreed she would. If she was 'okay' she wouldn't be looking at Rafe now as if he were a stranger to her rather than her lover.

She shrugged dismissively. 'Why wouldn't I be okay?'

Rafe didn't know the full answer to that; Dmitri Palitov hadn't been exactly forthcoming on the details yesterday, and would only reveal that Nina was upset about something he had told her, and had been missing since the previous night.

'Come inside.' Rafe kept a firm hold of her hand as he pulled her further into the room before shutting the door behind her. 'I can't tell you how pleased I am that you came here, Nina,' he added huskily.

'Why?'

Because now at least Rafe knew she was alive. Because now he knew she was safe.

Just because he needed her here with him, damn it.

'Nina, your father came to see me yesterday.'

Emotion flickered in the cool depths of those green eyes before it was quickly quashed. 'Did he?' she dismissed uninterestedly as she firmly but determinedly removed her hand from within Rafe's before walking away from him to stand in front of his desk. 'That must have been pleasant, for you both,' she added tersely.

Rafe continued to look at Nina searchingly, seeing the brittle fragility beneath her cool exterior. A fragility that was all the more apparent to him because she wore her hair up today, clearly revealing the hollows of her cheeks, the dark shadows beneath her eyes, and the delicate arch of her throat.

It was a fragility that Rafe believed might snap and break, shattering Nina along with it, if he said or did the wrong thing to her.

Which was the only reason Rafe hadn't taken Nina into his arms and kissed her senseless the moment he had closed the office door behind her.

Nina looked so brittle at the moment she was only capable of showing two responses to any attempt Rafe might make to hold her in his arms. One, she would fight him, biting and scratching with every bit of strength she possessed. Two, that fragile outer shell she held so tightly about her would crack wide open and she would disintegrate in front of his eyes. The first Rafe would withstand gladly, the second would utterly destroy him.

As it would destroy Nina.

And he didn't want that to happen. Nina's shy but rebellious spirit was one of the many things he had admired about her from the moment he first met her—was it really only a week ago?

That initial admiration had widened, and now included her unassuming beauty, her gentle sense of humour, her passion, the warmth of her heart, so evident when she spoke of her father.

A warmth so noticeably missing today whenever she spoke of Dmitri.

Rafe drew in a slow, measured breath, determined not to do or say anything that would shake the fragility of the tight control Nina had over her emotions. 'Nina…'

'I realise it would have been more businesslike to have made an appointment first, but I've brought in some sketches of my designs to show you,' she told him briskly, indicating the folder she carried in her left hand.

His brows rose at her use of the word 'businesslike'. 'Your designs?'

Her smile lacked any warmth or humour. 'I found myself with a lot of time on my hands over the weekend.'

Rafe winced.

Not only had Nina not spent the day with him yesterday, as he had hoped she would following the two of them spending the night together, but he also knew that after walking out of her father's apartment on Saturday evening Nina had gone down to her own apartment, packed a suitcase, and left the building altogether.

Because of something Dmitri had told her after they had returned home from the gala opening on Saturday evening. A conversation Nina had found so painful that she had apparently walked out of her father's apartment, swearing she would never forgive Dmitri for what he had done.

Quite what that was Rafe had no idea. Dmitri had remained close-mouthed about the details of that conversation when Rafe had repeatedly pressed him for answers. All Dmitri was interested in was finding Nina, and, as Rafe had shared that concern, the two men had reached an uneasy truce on the reasons for her disappearance.

Nor, it seemed, had Nina come to Rafe today for any other reason than to show him her designs.

When Rafe had been hoping she had come to be with him because she needed him.

As he needed her.

Rafe had been shocked yesterday to learn that Dmitri hadn't seen Nina since Saturday night either. Having discovered Nina was missing on Sunday morning, after eluding her security guards, Dmitri had gone straight to Rafe's apartment to look for her.

Only to learn that Rafe hadn't seen her since Saturday evening either.

Michael had walked in on the heated argument that followed as Rafe and Dmitri threw accusations at each other, out of their concern for Nina rather than any real anger towards each other. Having calmed the situation down enough to find out what the problem was, Michael had even offered to cancel his flight back to Paris in order to help them look for Nina. An offer Rafe had thanked him for but refused, knowing that he and Dmitri were the ones who had to look for her. Who had to find her. They had to ensure that she was safe.

The two men had spent most of yesterday calling any and all of Nina's friends or acquaintances to see if they had seen or heard from her. None of them had. Following that they had called hotel after hotel to see if a Nina Palitov had booked in late on Saturday night. When those calls had turned up nothing, they had widened the search to the suburbs, to any and all places Nina might have stayed since she had walked out on him.

All to no avail; Nina was out there somewhere, but she obviously didn't want to be found.

Rafe had hoped that didn't include by him, but her comment just now would seem to imply that she hadn't even been aware he would bother looking for her when she hadn't arrived at his apartment on Saturday night, as she had said she would. And maybe he deserved that dismissal; Nina had no way of knowing that Rafe had thought of little else but her since the moment he first met her.

And now, when she was hurting so badly, because of the things her father had told her, wasn't the right time for Rafe to tell her how he felt, either.

'You know, Nina...' he spoke softly '...whatever your father has done, whatever he's said to you, nothing and no one is ever as completely black or completely white as they appear, and those shady areas of grey can be—'

'Oh, please!' Nina cut him off disparagingly. 'He got to you, didn't he?' she continued with knowing derision. 'And no doubt he told you just enough to excuse his behaviour.'

'He told me nothing, Nina, made no excuses for whatever it was he's done to upset you,' Rafe assured gruffly.

'Because there aren't any!' Her eyes glittered deeply green as the first crack began to appear in her defensive shell, a lapse she quickly brought under control as she straightened her shoulders determinedly. 'There just aren't any excuses for what he did, Rafe,' she repeated evenly.

'He loves you very much. He was only trying to protect you.'

'He's protected me from life all of my life!' Angry colour appeared in the pallor of her cheeks.

'Yes, he has,' Rafe acknowledged gently. 'And maybe that was wrong of him.'

'Maybe?' She moved restlessly. 'There's no maybe about it!' Her eyes continued to glitter angrily. 'He must have told you something, Rafe,' she continued scornfully. 'Enough that he's the one you feel sorry for, obviously.'

'It isn't a question of feeling sorry for anyone.'

'Isn't it?' she dismissed harshly. 'Well, believe me, I don't feel in the least sorry for him after hearing the things he's kept from me all these years.'

Rafe looked at her searchingly, the glitter of tears in her eyes enough to tell him that she wasn't as immune to her father's pain as she claimed to be. 'This isn't really you, Nina,' he cajoled huskily. 'You love your father, and you don't have it in you to be deliberately cruel, to him or anyone else.'

She gave another humourless laugh. 'What do you really know about me, Rafe? That I like having your hands on me? That I liked it so much on Saturday evening I let you drag me into a damned cupboard full of brooms just so that you could pleasure me?' She gave a disgusted shake of her head. 'That isn't knowing me, Rafe, that's just enjoying having sex.'

'Don't,' he warned harshly, knowing exactly what she was going to say next, and totally unwilling to allow her to reduce what they had to that basic level. 'You came to me today, Nina,' he reminded her gruffly, hands clenched at his sides to prevent himself from reaching out and taking her in his arms. 'Whatever excuse you may have given yourself for coming here, you came to me, damn it!'

Yes, she had, Nina acknowledged heavily. This morning, as she'd showered and dressed in her hotel room, she had convinced herself she was going to see Rafe today because she wanted the commission for the display cabinets from Archangel galleries. That securing those designs was more important than her pride if she was really serious about launching her own design company.

Now that she was here, with Rafe, Nina wasn't so sure she had been altogether truthful, even to herself.

There was comfort for her in being in Rafe's company, in that quiet strength he had, and it was already acting as a balm to her shattered emotions. It fed the need she felt to be with someone who desired her, at least, and who could warm her even a little; at the moment her heart felt like a heavy block of ice in her chest.

So, yes, she had come to Rafe this morning, had needed, wanted to be with him. To be with the man she had realised that she had fallen in love with.

Not all of the last thirty-six hours had been spent thinking about that last conversation with her father. She had thought of Rafe too. A lot. Of what their relationship meant to her. Of the fact that she not only desired and wanted him, but that she liked him too. That she had fallen in love with him.

Her desire for Rafe's dark good looks was undeniable, and she liked that fun person he could so often be, but she also knew, after this past week, that there was so much more to Rafe than that charming rogue persona he chose to show to the world at large.

Rafe cared.

About the Archangel galleries.

About her…

And he loved his family deeply. And it was a love, after her conversation with Michael on Saturday evening, which she had no doubts his family returned.

The serious Michael had made a point of talking to her

alone about his brother Rafe, casually at first, and then of how hard and diligently Rafe worked for the success of the galleries, of how they all owed much of the galleries' continued success to Rafe's ideas and innovations.

It was a caring part of Rafe that had already shone through bright and clear to Nina no matter how hard he tried to hide it.

Enough that she had already fallen in love with him.

A love that Rafe would never return.

She straightened her shoulders determinedly. 'The only reason I'm here today is to show you my designs,' she assured him coolly. 'If you're still interested in seeing them, that is?'

'Nina, we can't just sit down together and discuss your designs as if your conversation with your father on Saturday night had never happened.'

'I don't see why not,' she cut in icily.

'Nina—'

'Exactly what did he tell you about that conversation, Rafe?' she prompted again, harshly. 'How much of the truth, having known you for a week and me my whole lifetime, did he decide to confide in you?'

Rafe straightened, his tone soothing. 'You have to calm down, Nina.'

'No, Rafe, I really don't. I don't have to do anything, not any more.' Her eyes had a reckless glow. 'From now on I intend to do exactly as I damn well please. Now, do you want to see my designs or not?'

He winced at the aggression in her tone. 'Of course I want to see your designs.'

'Then could we do it now, please?' She handed him the file. 'I have business premises and an apartment to find this afternoon.'

'You aren't returning to your own apartment?' He frowned.

Her jaw tightened. 'No.'

Rafe was at a complete loss to know how to deal with this hard, unreachable Nina. He barely recognised her as the woman who had occupied most of his waking thoughts this past week—and quite a few of his sleeping ones too.

The woman he only had to look at to feel aroused. The woman who teased him and made him laugh. A woman of warmth and gentleness. A woman he had confided in. A woman so unlike any other that Rafe felt beguiled by her. The woman he knew he wanted to be with.

The same woman who was hurting so badly right now she was falling apart inside.

Because whatever Dmitri had told her on Saturday night it hurt her. Deeply.

Rafe didn't know all the facts—no matter what Nina might think, Dmitri really hadn't been willing to go quite so far as to confide in him—but Rafe knew enough to know that whatever secrets the other man had been keeping from Nina all these years it was breaking her apart.

If it hadn't already broken her heart.

'Nina—'

'Please, Rafe.' Her voice cracked emotionally. 'If you care anything for me at all, then help me do this.'

If Rafe cared?

He had realised, during these past two days that he cared more for Nina, about Nina, than he ever had for any woman. Than he ever would again for any woman. 'Nina...'

Both of them turned as the door to his office was suddenly thrown open without warning. Rafe groaned inwardly as the two burly bodyguards entered the room before parting to allow Dmitri Palitov to enter in his wheelchair.

One look at Nina's white and accusing face, and Rafe knew that she believed he'd had something to do with her father's unexpected arrival.

CHAPTER ELEVEN

'DID YOU INSTRUCT your assistant to inform my father if I came here?' Nina looked at him with hurt accusation.

'No.'

'Rafe has absolutely nothing to do with my being here this morning, Nina.' Dmitri spoke quietly, the two bodyguards once again instructed to wait out in the hallway, the door firmly closed behind them. 'I've had both Rafe's apartment and this gallery under observation since yesterday, on the off-chance that you might come to him.'

Rafe scowled darkly. 'You have one hell of a nerve!'

Which wasn't to say, despite the outrage Rafe felt now on Nina's behalf, that he didn't still feel a certain inner warmth in the knowledge that, whatever reason she claimed for being here today, Nina had come to him.

'My apologies, Rafe. But it was necessary,' the older man added.

'In your opinion,' Nina snapped, though she was relieved that Rafe hadn't had anything to do with her father being here. She wasn't sure she was strong enough to face another betrayal by one of the two men who meant so much to her.

Her father looked at her calmly. 'Where have you been for the past two days, Nina?'

'Right here at a hotel in New York.'

'We checked all the hotels.'

'I booked in under the name Nina Fraser,' she said, feeling no sense of satisfaction as she saw the way her father flinched at hearing she had booked into the hotel using her mother's maiden name.

She was hurt and angry with her father, yes, for the things he had kept from her, but Rafe was right, she wasn't, and never could be, deliberately cruel to anyone, least of all her father. 'You should have told me the truth about Mama from the beginning, Papa,' she said softly.

A spasm of pain passed over his already strained features. 'You were only five years old, and far too young to understand, let alone accept that truth.'

'But later, you should have tried to explain it to me when I was older,' she came back emotionally.

'I thought of it, of course I did. But it was not pleasant, *maya doch*.' Her father looked haggard. 'Better, I decided, that you had the good memories of your mama and not the bad.'

Rafe had no idea what the two of them were talking about, but that didn't prevent him from feeling as if he was intruding on something very personal to the two of them. 'Perhaps you would like me to leave so the two of you can talk privately?'

'No.'

'No!'

Rafe nodded as both Palitovs spoke at the same time, Dmitri with resignation, Nina with an edge of desperation. And if Nina needed him to be here, then that was exactly where Rafe was going to be.

'Let's sit down, shall we, Nina?' Rafe encouraged gently, sitting down beside her as she perched on the edge of the sofa.

Nina gave Rafe a quick glance as he lifted one of her

trembling hands to lace his fingers with hers, a wave of gratitude sweeping over her at this tacit show of his support. Overwhelming love for him bubbled up, swelled to overflowing inside her, for the gentleness Rafe showed towards her.

Because Nina now knew, beyond a shadow of a doubt, that she did love Rafe, that she was in love with him.

Which was why, much as she might have protested at the thought of Rafe leaving a few minutes ago, she now had to be fair to him and give him a chance to do exactly that.

'I'm aware this is your office, Rafe, and I'm sorry for the way we've intruded.' She spoke quietly. 'But you really don't have to be here to listen to this if you would rather not.' She looked up, appealing to her father.

He understood her silent plea as he gave a slight nod before turning to the younger man. 'You may prefer not to be here, Rafe.'

'I want whatever Nina wants.' Rafe's expression gentled as he turned to look at her, once again noting the tension she was under, how the shadows seemed to have deepened in those deep green eyes. 'I want to be here for you,' he told her huskily. 'If it's what you want too?'

'Yes, please,' she breathed.

He nodded before turning back to Dmitri. 'Then I'm staying right here,' he told the older man firmly.

Nina's fingers tightened about his in gratitude before she turned to look at her father with tear-wet eyes. 'It was cruel of you to keep the truth about Mama from me all these years, Papa. Surely I had a right to know? A right to choose for myself?'

'I did what I thought was best at the time.' He sighed heavily. 'And this conversation must be very confusing for Rafe,' he added. 'Which, as we are in his office, seems a little unfair.'

The tears were falling silently down Nina's cheeks as she turned to Rafe. 'It's not too late, you can still leave.'

'I'm staying,' he stated grimly, wanting, needing, to know exactly what had reduced his Nina to this emotional state.

She drew in a deep breath. 'Then you should know that nineteen years ago my mother was kidnapped.' She nodded abruptly at Rafe's harshly indrawn breath. 'The kidnappers contacted my father immediately, demanding that he keep the police out of it, but that if he paid their ransom within one week my mother would be safely returned to us.'

Now Rafe understood the reason Dmitri Palitov had been, and still was, so protective of his daughter; his wife had been taken from him nineteen years ago, and he had no intention of the same thing ever happening with his young daughter.

Rafe felt a hard jolt in his chest just imagining how Dmitri must have suffered all those years ago. The pain and agony of having his wife taken from him followed by days of wondering if he would ever see her again.

Imagining how he himself would feel if it had been Nina!

The knuckles on Nina's hands showed white as she held on tightly, painfully, to Rafe's hand. 'My father obeyed their instructions, paid the men their ransom, but—but—'

'This is where our stories start to diverge,' Dmitri put in softly, heavily, as Nina faltered. 'At the time I told Nina nothing about the kidnapping, only that Anna had died. And then when Nina was ten years old I told her of the kidnapping, as a way of helping her to understand why I was so protective of her, but not— Until Saturday evening I was still not completely truthful about her mother's fate.'

Rafe looked at the older man searchingly, eyes widening in shock as he read the truth in Dmitri's agonised expression. 'Anna didn't die when Nina was five,' he breathed, remembering how he hadn't been able to find any record of Anna's death when he did an Internet search on Dmitri Palitov.

Dmitri's jaw tightened. 'Anna died five years later, in the private nursing home I had been forced to place her in just days after she was returned to me. She is buried in the churchyard nearby. Her mind had gone, you see, so that she no longer knew me. She had retreated to a place neither I nor anyone else could reach her, for ever broken from what those animals did to her in the week they held her captive.'

'Don't, Papa!' Nina choked emotionally, reaching out to him with her other hand, aware of the cracking of the ice that had encased her heart since she had learnt the truth two days ago.

That ice now broke wide open, shattered completely, before melting away as she saw the agony of that shocking past in her father's pained green eyes.

It had been too much for Nina to take in on Saturday night, for her to be able to fully comprehend what his having kept that secret all these years had done to her father, emotionally. All she had heard then, all that had mattered, was that her mother had been alive for five years more after Nina had believed her to be dead.

But she realised, as she looked at her father now, how alone he must have been in his grieving for the wife who had never completely come back to him. Of the five years he had suffered, visiting Anna once a week at the nursing home where she had lived out the rest of her short life, so lost in the safety of the world she had created for herself that she hadn't even known who Dmitri was, let alone that she had a young daughter who loved her too.

And Nina realised now that he had done that for her. So that she might grow up with only the happy memories of her mother.

'It was wrong of me.'

'Don't put yourself through having to say it all again, Papa!' Nina pleaded emotionally. 'It isn't. I was the one who was wrong on Saturday evening, for not understanding.' She released Rafe's hand so that she could stand up to go to her father, her arms moving about him protectively as the tears now trailed down his weathered cheeks.

'I'm so sorry, Papa. So very sorry that I walked out on you on Saturday night. For putting you through yet more pain by disappearing for two days.'

'I would forgive you anything, *maya doch*, you know that.' He spoke gruffly. 'Anything, as long as you are safe.'

Nina began to cry in earnest now, no longer able to shut out the thought of all the years her father had suffered, unable to share or express his grief for the wife who still lived but no longer had any knowledge of him or their young daughter.

'There's more, isn't there?'

Nina kept her arms protectively about her father as she turned to look across at Rafe.

'Not that this isn't already enough.' Rafe stood up abruptly, too restless to continue sitting any longer.

His hands were clenched at his sides as he resisted the impulse he had to take Nina in his own arms, knowing that this was a time of understanding, of healing, for Nina and Dmitri. A time when Rafe's own emotions had to be kept firmly in check. Which wasn't to say he didn't feel them.

He gave a shake of his head. 'I can't even begin to tell you how sorry I am that this happened to all of you. It's incomprehensible. Too huge to take in completely.' He ran a hand through the shaggy thickness of his hair as he gave a shake of his head, wondering how Dmitri had ever managed to live with the pain.

Rafe had grown up in the security of the deep love his own parents had for each other, and he knew, without a doubt, without needing to ask, that his own father would have acted in exactly the same way Dmitri had in these same circumstances. That having lost his wife, Giorgio would have done everything in his considerable power to care for his wife, and ensure his three sons were protected from the truth.

Rafe also knew that Gabriel, so in love with Bryn, would tear the world apart looking for anyone who dared to hurt her.

Just as Rafe knew, if that had ever happened to him, that once the initial shock had receded he would be filled with that same rage. That he would want to find the men responsible, to destroy them, to tear them apart with his bare hands, for what they had done to the woman he loved, and to make sure they were never able to hurt another woman, to destroy another family in the way that they had.

He drew in a hissing breath. 'Your car accident wasn't an accident, was it?'

'No,' the older man confirmed as he drew himself up stiffly while retaining a tight hold of Nina's hand. 'It took time, but I hunted the three kidnappers down until I found them, and then I arranged to meet with them.' He drew in a controlling breath. 'It was my intention to kill them that night, at a secluded spot far from the city, to make them suffer, as my Anna had suffered—' He broke off as Nina gave a pained cry. 'I did not succeed, *maya doch*,' he assured her huskily.

'You didn't?' Nina gasped. 'But all these years I've thought—believed— We never spoke of it openly, but I always assumed…?'

Dmitri gave a rueful shake of his head. 'It would seem they had the same intention in regard to me. They did not wish to have anyone left alive who could identify them.' His jaw tightened. 'They rammed my car on the way to that meeting, attempted to drive my car off the road. Instead it was their own car which bore the brunt of the impact.' His mouth tightened. 'Two of the men were killed instantly, the third died a year later, as a result of the injuries he had received.' Dmitri made the statement evenly, unemotionally, and with no apology for what he had intended.

As far as Rafe was concerned no apology was necessary. Dmitri had done what he felt he had to do. What most men would have done in the same situation.

What Rafe would have wanted to do given those same circumstances.

'I think,' Rafe spoke slowly, 'that if I had known you then, Dmitri, young as I was, that I would have wanted to help you in your search for the kidnappers.'

Nina felt so grateful to Rafe at that moment, for not judging, for not condemning her father for what he had intended, that she could have kissed him!

She wanted to kiss him anyway. Had been longing, aching, to do exactly that since the moment she had entered his office half an hour earlier.

Just as she had longed to go to Rafe on Saturday night, despite the things her father had told her. She had needed

Rafe then, had been desperate to feel his arms about her, to lose herself in their lovemaking rather than dwell on those lost years with her mother.

But she had known instinctively that it was the wrong thing to do.

Knew that if Rafe ever learned the details of the conversation she'd had with her father he would feel she had been using him that night, rather than what was true— that she had just ached to be with him, to be held by him that night. Because she loved him.

'You are an impressive young man, Raphael D'Angelo.' Dmitri spoke appreciatively.

Rafe raised dark brows. 'I happen to think your daughter is the impressive one.' He looked at Nina with open admiration. 'All these years she's secretly wondered if you killed those men that night, and yet she's held her own counsel, never speaking of it to anyone.'

'Yes.' Dmitri's pride glowed in his eyes for his daughter.

Nina winced. 'Maybe if I'd spoken to my father about it before now I wouldn't have been left secretly wondering. I feel so ashamed now, for thinking what I did, Papa. I'm sorry. I really believed—thought that…'

'It was only fate that decreed it otherwise, *maya doch*,' her father soothed gently. 'I left our apartment that night with every intention of ridding the world of those three men.'

'But you didn't do it.' She clasped her father's hands tightly in hers as that truth finally sank in completely, Nina feeling as if a weight had been lifted from her shoulders. 'You didn't do it, Papa!' And that weight lifted even higher as she realised what that knowledge meant to her own life, and the freedom, the choices it now gave her.

'No, I did not,' he conceded gruffly. 'Because as I

drove to the meeting point that night I realised that I could not do it. Because of you, Nina.' He squeezed her hand. 'Much as I wished to rid the world of such vermin as those men, I would then have had to pay for my crime, and so left you completely alone. And that I could not do, *maya doch*. I could not leave you without both your mother and your father.'

Tears blurred Nina's vision as she wept silently.

Tears for the deep love her father felt for her, and which she returned.

Tears of joy because she now knew her suspicions all these years, regarding who had been responsible for her father's accident, and the deaths of those three men, had been wrong.

Tears for the freedom that knowledge now gave her in her own life, allowing her to give her heart, her love, to the man she was already so deeply in love with.

It didn't matter that Rafe would never return that love; it was enough that Nina could now allow herself, was finally free, to be with him for as long as he wanted her.

If he still wanted her?

Rafe felt a jolt in his chest as Nina turned to smile at him. A smile of such sweet, unadulterated joy that he had to blink as it made his own eyes sting with emotion.

But there was still one question Dmitri had left unanswered.

'Why now, Dmitri?' he prompted huskily as he turned to look at the other man. 'Why did you decide now was the right time to tell Nina the truth about her mother?'

The older man smiled up at him sadly. 'Why do you think, Rafe?'

Rafe looked at Dmitri searchingly, not sure, uncertain still—

But he could hope, couldn't he?

Yes, he could certainly hope that this was Dmitri's way of letting Nina go. Of allowing her to have her own life at last. Of allowing her to live. To love.

Because Dmitri had realised, already knew, that Rafe was in love with her.

'I realise that you and Nina still have a lot to discuss, Dmitri.' He spoke huskily to the older man while all the time turning to look at Nina. 'But would you mind very much if I were to steal her away for a few hours? I very much doubt she's bothered to eat very much the last two days, so I could feed her lunch at least,' he added ruefully as he saw Nina's puzzled glance.

'I think that would be an excellent idea, Rafe.' Dmitri nodded. 'And Nina and I have the rest of our lives in which to talk more of all these things.'

'Nina?' Rafe prompted as he held his hand out to her, holding his breath as he waited for her response.

CHAPTER TWELVE

'DID YOU NOTICE that my father stopped Andy and Rich as they moved to follow us?'

Rafe glanced at Nina as she sat beside him in the passenger seat of his car, looking so vulnerable and young at that moment, her eyes slightly red from where she had cried earlier, her face completely bare of make-up.

'I did, yes.'

'It's really going to be okay, isn't it?' she murmured shakily.

Rafe reached out to briefly squeeze her hand before returning his own hand to the steering wheel. 'Yes, it's really going to be okay.'

She relaxed back against the leather seat. 'I'm sorry you had to listen to all of that.'

'I didn't have to do anything, Nina, I chose to do it,' he corrected firmly. 'And I think it's time you stopped apologising. To me. To your father. Or to anyone else. Because you have absolutely nothing to apologise for.' He glanced at her again, and saw the frown between those beautiful emerald-coloured eyes. 'Do you have any idea how much I admire you right now?'

Rafe admired her?

It wasn't exactly the return of her love that Nina longed

for, she acknowledged ruefully, but it was high praise indeed coming from the enigmatic Rafe D'Angelo.

'That's nice,' she accepted huskily.

'Nice?' he echoed dryly.

'Very nice?' She quirked a teasing brow, happier than she had ever been at this moment, just knowing there were no more misunderstandings, nothing left unsaid, between her and her father.

More importantly, she was with Rafe. The man she loved. A love that had grown deeper, even stronger, during this past hour as he gave her his strength to lean on.

Those chiselled lips twisted laughingly. 'The first time I tell a woman I admire her, and all she can say is, "That's nice,"' he muttered disgustedly.

'I did expand it to very nice,' Nina reminded lightly, desperately trying not to read any more into his statement than Rafe actually meant. Because it would be all too easy for her to do exactly that, and the last thing Nina wanted to do was embarrass Rafe, or herself, by overreacting to his comment. 'Isn't admiration something you feel for talcum-powder-smelling maiden aunts?'

He frowned. 'I don't have any maiden aunts!'

'That explains why you've never said it before, then.' She nodded.

'Exactly where are we going for lunch?' She changed the subject to something less open to misunderstandings. Or hope, on her part, not Rafe's.

Rafe bit back his feelings of impatience with Nina's determination to keep their conversation lightly teasing.

He might have received Dmitri's tacit approval just minutes ago, but it was too soon for Rafe to expect, to ask, for anything from Nina other than the physical attraction between them that she had never tried to deny.

He sensed that was all Nina needed from him right now: to be able to lose herself in desire, passion and pleasure.

'To the best restaurant in New York,' he answered her lightly.

'Am I dressed appropriately?' She looked down uncertainly at the business suit she had worn to his office this morning. Like a suit of armour.

'I thought we might go to my apartment. Do you think you're dressed appropriately for there?' Rafe prompted huskily.

Nina's cheeks flushed a fiery red as she recalled that the last time she'd been in Rafe's apartment she'd been completely naked! 'I didn't know you could cook?'

'I can't,' he admitted unapologetically. 'It will just be fruit and cheese, I'm afraid. It's where we're going to eat the food from that's going to make it the best restaurant in town.'

The warmth deepened in her cheeks. 'Would you care to enlighten me?'

'Oh, I'd care to do a lot of things to and with you, Nina,' Rafe assured huskily as he parked the car in the private underground parking beneath his apartment building, before turning in his seat to look at her. 'First I want to strip you naked. Second I want to lay you down on my bed before arranging my lunch on selected parts of your delectable body. Thirdly I want to then taste, lick, nibble each tiny morsel of pleasure.'

'Rafe!' Nina gasped breathlessly, her heart leaping in her chest just thinking of the intimacies he'd described.

He reached up to release the clasp from her hair, allowing it to cascade loosely onto her shoulders and down her spine. 'Too much?' he prompted huskily.

Not enough! It would never be enough for her where Rafe was concerned.

But this, here and now, with Rafe, anticipating the lovemaking yet to come, was exactly what she needed after the last two emotionally traumatic days.

'Do I get to eat my lunch in the same way?'

He quirked one dark brow. 'Do you want to?'

'Oh, yes,' she breathed longingly.

Rafe nodded. 'I'm starving for you,' he murmured huskily, his golden gaze easily holding hers captive. 'How about you?'

Nina moistened the softness of her lips before answering. 'Ravenous.'

'Thank God!' he groaned his satisfaction with her answer before getting out of the car and moving quickly round to her side of the vehicle to open her door for her, taking a firm hold of her elbow as they crossed the car park to the lift.

The lift doors had barely closed behind them before Rafe took her in his arms and kissed her. Deeply, hungrily, as if he couldn't get enough of her. As if it was her he wanted to eat and to hell with lunch!

They were still kissing greedily as they stepped out of the lift into Rafe's apartment. Their lips locked together as they hurriedly threw off their clothes, moving erratically towards Rafe's bedroom, clothes left scattered down the hallway, both of them completely naked by the time they fell on the bed together and they lost themselves in the pleasure of each other.

'So much for lunch,' Nina murmured a long time later, fingers toying with the damp vee of dark hair on Rafe's muscled chest and abdomen as they lay entwined together between the silk sheets.

'Oh, we're still going to eat lunch, Nina,' Rafe assured her huskily, his hair rakishly tousled as he moved up onto his elbow to look down at her, thoroughly enjoying seeing the satisfied glow in her eyes, the flush to her cheeks, her lips lush and full, and her hair a wild and silky red tangle. 'I just—I needed you too much this first time to be able to take things slowly,' he acknowledged gruffly.

Her eyes widened. 'You did?'

'I did,' he admitted. 'I wasn't too rough with you, was I?' He lightly caressed the dampness of her hair back from her temple.

'Not at all.' She smiled shyly. 'Was I too rough with you?'

'Not at all,' Rafe echoed softly. 'Nina—' He broke off to chew uncertainly on his bottom lip.

'Yes?' she prompted curiously. The Rafe she knew and loved was never uncertain, always seemed to know exactly what he was doing, and why.

He drew in a deep and ragged breath. 'I promised myself I wasn't going to do this today, that you've had enough trauma for one day...'

Nina's stomach tied up in tense knots as she looked up at him searchingly, as she wondered if the intensity of Rafe's lovemaking just now hadn't been because, for him, this was the end of their relationship.

If it was, then she would accept his decision, had no intention of making Rafe feel in the least guilty about ending their affair. He had been there for her this morning when she had needed him, so strong and so kind. He'd listened without judgement as her father talked of the past, and at the same time been totally supportive of her. So much so that the least Nina owed him was to make a dignified exit from his life, if that was what he wanted.

'You don't want to see me any more,' she accepted lightly.

'What?' Rafe's face tensed. His eyes had darkened to molten gold, his skin taut across the sharp blades of his cheekbones, nostrils flaring, his lips having compressed to a thin, uncompromising line.

'It's okay, Rafe.' She touched his chest lightly, reassuringly, determined to remain strong. There would be plenty of time later for her to break down. As her heart was already breaking at the thought of not being with Rafe like this again. 'I knew going into this that you don't do long-term relationships. Or complications,' she added ruefully. 'And it seems that my life is just one shocking complication after another!'

Rafe scowled darkly. 'You don't want to be with me any more?'

'You don't want to be with me!' she corrected emotionally.

'I didn't say that,' he rasped harshly.

'But...' Nina frowned up at him. 'It sounded as if you did.'

'Absolutely not!' Rafe threw back the bed sheet to climb restlessly out of bed, unconcerned by his nakedness as he began to pace the bedroom, at the same time as he ran an agitated hand through the unruly darkness of his hair. 'The timing of this is all wrong,' he muttered crossly.

'The timing of what is all wrong?' Nina looked completely baffled by his behaviour.

Rafe gave an impatient shake of his head. 'You're naturally upset, traumatised after learning your mother lived.'

'Rafe, I'm fine,' she cut in gently. 'I really am,' she assured huskily as Rafe stopped pacing long enough to look across the bedroom at her. 'In fact, I'm better than I've ever been,' she added ruefully as she also threw back the bed sheet and climbed out of bed. 'I know the truth now, all of it. Don't you see, Rafe, for the first time in years I feel free of the emotional baggage I've been carrying about with me for most of my life?'

'Free to do what?' Rafe prompted searchingly, trying his damnedest not to be distracted by the beauty of Nina's nakedness. A battle he knew he was destined to lose as he became instantly aroused. For Nina. Only for Nina.

'To live. To love,' she added huskily as her gaze seemed drawn, as if by a magnet, to the physical evidence of Rafe's rapidly lengthening arousal.

Rafe's breath caught in his throat as he couldn't look away from the provocation of seeing Nina's little pink tongue sweep moistly across the plumpness of her bottom lip. As if in anticipation of licking him!

He wasn't even aware of having stepped towards her until he realised he was now standing only inches away from her, not quite touching her, but wanting to. Dear God, how much he wanted to just take Nina in his arms and make love to her again, to keep her in his arms, in his bed, until she promised never to leave.

He swallowed before speaking. 'I'm in love with you, Nina.' He gruffly spoke the words he had never imagined he would ever say to any woman, but desperately needing to say them now, to Nina, more than he needed his next breath.

'I love you.' It was much easier saying it the second time, something seeming to lighten, to ease deep inside Rafe, a heaviness, a restraint, he hadn't even known was there until it lifted.

'I love you, Nina Palitov,' he murmured again with satisfaction as he took her into his arms at last and curved the heat of his body against hers. 'I love you, Nina. I love you. I love you!' His voice rose joyfully as he announced his love for her over and over again, knowing he would never grow tired of saying it.

Nina stared up at Rafe wonderingly, almost afraid still to believe, to hope that he was saying these wonderful words to her when just seconds ago she had thought he was saying goodbye.

'I love you too,' she breathed softly. 'I love you too, Rafe.' She spoke more strongly now too as her hands moved up to rest on the warmth of his chest, allowing her to feel the wild beating of his heart beneath her fingertips.

Rafe's arms tightened about her.

'Marry me, Nina,' he urged forcefully. 'Marry me!' His eyes blazed fiercely down into hers.

She stared up at him unblinkingly. 'Raphael D'Angelo doesn't do love and marriage.'

'He didn't do love and marriage,' he corrected gruffly. 'Until you. But you should know right now that I'm not going to settle for anything less when it comes to you.' His arms tightened about her. 'I want you for always, Nina. As my wife. As the mother of my babies. God, just thinking of you pregnant with our child makes me hard!' he acknowledged huskily as his arousal surged against her. 'I want a lifetime with you, Nina. Want to wake up beside you every morning, to have the freedom to be able to tell you how much I love you a dozen times a day!'

Nina gazed up at him wonderingly. 'Yes, Rafe. Oh, yes, of course I'll marry you!' Her arms moved about his waist. 'I love you so much. So very much, Rafe!' She raised her face to meet the fierce possessiveness of his kiss.

The rest of the world drifted away, ceased to exist, as they revelled in the depth of the love they had found with and for each other.

* * * * *

A sneaky peek at next month...

MODERN™

POWER, PASSION AND IRRESISTIBLE TEMPTATION

My wish list for next month's titles...

In stores from 21st March 2014:

❏ A D'Angelo Like No Other – Carole Mortimer

❏ When Christakos Meets His Match – Abby Green

❏ Secrets of a Bollywood Marriage – Susanna Carr

❏ The Last Prince of Dahaar – Tara Pammi

In stores from 4th April 2014:

❏ Seduced by the Sultan – Sharon Kendrick

❏ The Purest of Diamonds? – Susan Stephens

❏ What the Greek's Money Can't Buy – Maya Blake

❏ The Sicilian's Unexpected Duty – Michelle Smart

Available at WHSmith, Tesco, Asda, Eason, Amazon and Apple

Just can't wait?

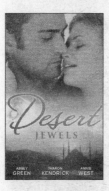

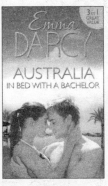
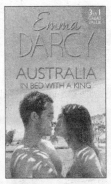
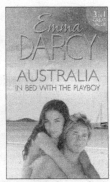
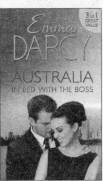
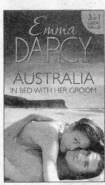
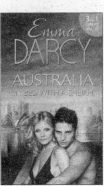

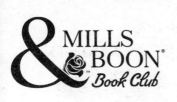

Join the Mills & Boon Book Club

Subscribe to **Modern**™ today for 3, 6 or 12 months and you could **save over £40!**

We'll also treat you to these fabulous extras:

- 🌹 **FREE L'Occitane gift set worth £10**
- 🌹 **FREE home delivery**
- 🌹 **Rewards scheme, exclusive offers...and much more!**

Subscribe now and save over £40
www.millsandboon.co.uk/subscribeme

SUBS/OFFER/P1

Discover more romance at

www.millsandboon.co.uk

- ❤ WIN great prizes in our exclusive competitions
- ❤ BUY new titles before they hit the shops
- ❤ BROWSE new books and REVIEW your favourites
- ❤ SAVE on new books with the Mills & Boon® Bookclub™
- ❤ DISCOVER new authors

PLUS, to chat about your favourite reads, get the latest news and find special offers:

- f Find us on facebook.com/millsandboon
- ➤ Follow us on twitter.com/millsandboonuk
- ❤ Sign up to our newsletter at millsandboon.co.uk